ALPHA'S CHALLENGE

AN MC WEREWOLF ROMANCE

RENEE ROSE
LEE SAVINO

Midnight
ROMANCE

Published in the United States of America

Renee Rose Romance and Silverwood Press and Midnight Romance, LLC

Editor: Kate Richards

Wizards in Publishing

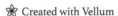 Created with Vellum

WANT FREE BOOKS?

Go to reneeroseromance.com to sign up for Renee Rose's newsletter and receive a free copy of *Theirs to Protect, Owned by the Marine, Theirs to Punish, The Alpha's Punishment, Disobedience at the Dressmaker's* and *Her Billionaire Boss.* In addition to the free stories, you will also get special pricing, exclusive previews and news of new releases.

Go to www.leesavino.com to sign up for Lee Savino's awesomesauce mailing list and get a FREE Berserker book —too hot to publish anywhere else!

ACKNOWLEDGMENTS

A huge thank you to our wonderful 11th hour beta readers, Katherine Deane and Aubrey Cara, and to Margarita C. for her legal help and advice.

Huge smooches to Kate Richards, our fabulous editor, who always makes us read better and squeezes our books in-between holidays and other projects when we're on a hard deadline, and to Miranda, aka Mommy's a Book Whore, for extra editing and beta reading.

Thank you to Lee's Goddess Group and Renee's Romper Room for your support and love. Thanks to our ARC readers and to L. Woods PR and the bloggers who support our releases. You are all amazing!

1

F *oxfire*

A SMALL POP is my only warning before my soup explodes.

"Dammit." I rip open the microwave door. Only half my tomato soup is left, and the inside of my microwave looks like a murder scene.

Good thing I already ordered a pizza.

With a sigh, I shut the door on the gruesome red spatter. My stomach's gurgling like I haven't eaten in a day. Maybe I haven't. I barely know what day it is. Day Eight of the Breakup From Hell, and the only thing keeping me connected to the outside world is my best friend.

Speaking of best friends...I hit my one and only speed dial number. It goes straight to voicemail, catching me by surprise. Amber should be home, lying low after I rescued her from her own date from hell.

I give up the call and shoot off a text, *Just ordered a pizza —come share half?*

It's probably too soon to mention her dating disaster. She'd only known the guy a few days, but he was her neighbor. *Awkward.* And yeah, he was hot, but since when does that give a guy an excuse to abandon a woman on the side of a mountain in the middle of a first date?

My ex is a jackhole, and even he wouldn't do that.

Bring a picture of Garrett. I've got one of Benny, and a bunch of darts... I start to text and delete it. Instead, I type, *I'm giving up on men forever. Let's get fat and adopt lots of cats.*

There. That'll make her laugh.

I pace around the house, noting piles of mail and takeout detritus that appeared over the past few days. Since the breakup, I've been practically a hermit. Benny still hasn't come by, even to pick up his stuff.

Not that I want him to. Rat bastard.

Amber still hasn't texted me back. Weird. It's six p.m. on a Saturday night, but my best friend is usually home, alone. Like me.

Geez, we're pathetic. Maybe we really should adopt some cats.

I text Amber again. *Don't adopt any cats without me.*

My mom was right. Men suck. I'll be happy if I never see another man for the rest of my life. Except the pizza delivery guy. I'll make an exception for him.

When the doorbell rings, I dash out to the living room and open it, perhaps a wee bit too eagerly.

"What do I owe..." My voice dies. I look up. And up. And up some more.

Damn, this pizza delivery boy is tall. And stacked. Like The Rock or something. Six-foot and then some, with shoulders almost too big for the door. Military buzz cut. Mirrored shades on his face... at dusk.

Hey ,big boy, my foxy bits purr. No! Bad Foxfire!

"Foxfire Hines?" He looks a bit disbelieving, like he can't quite believe that's my name. I get that a lot.

"My mother is a hippie," I say.

"What?" His eyebrows shoot up over the shades.

"My name. It's because... my mom is a hippie. She thought it was pretty."

"Your mom?"

"Yes."

"Your name is really Foxfire?" He sounds almost resigned, like he can't believe the turn his life has taken, to deliver him to my door. I understand. I've never pledged my undying lust to a pizza guy. Both of us are having a night of firsts.

"Were you waiting for me?" he asks.

"Uh, yeah." Then it hits me, through the cloud of longing. What my brain was screaming over my libido. "Wait... where's the pizza?"

~.~

Tank

FOXFIRE. Fucking ridiculous. The chick looks as crazy as her name. On paper, she's okay. Graphic designer, good client list, pays her bills on time. Lives in a respectable adobe brick house near the university. So far, so good. In person, she's a walking, talking freak show. Hair is dyed like a rainbow, something out of a cartoon. She's also tiny, a petite pixie in short shorts and strappy tank. I could pick her up and hold her in my hand.

Oh, and she's stunning. Even with the clown hair.

This job's either gonna be easy or a huge pain in my ass.

"Where's the pizza?" She peers around me. Before she can protest, I push inside, noting the explosion of papers on every surface, bean bag chairs on the floor, a few dream catchers in the windows, and a lava lamp in the corner. The cartoon pixie lives in La La Land.

"What are you doing?" She blinks at me, her starry eyes wide. Totally unafraid. A man twice her size just pushed into her house, and she's asking about pizza. Most women would be freaked.

Not this one.

Like I said, La La Land.

"I need to talk to you," I say.

"Okay." She adds in a hopeful tone, "Did you leave the pizza in the car?"

"No pizza. This is about Amber."

"Amber?" Her head snaps back, and she sucks in a breath.

"Miss Hines, you better sit down."

To my surprise, she drops onto the only decent seat in the place, a battered couch. She responded to my authority right away. If she was pack, I'd say she was a feisty but submissive wolf.

Maybe this is going to be easy.

"Is something wrong? Is Amber in trouble?"

"Not yet. Not if you cooperate."

"What?" she whispers, the blood draining from her face.

The scent of her fear fills the room, and my wolf raises his head. Because he fucking *hates* it.

It's my turn to suck in a breath. My wolf never pays any attention to humans. Not even pretty females with freaky hair.

"I'm not here to hurt you." Now, why did I promise that? I'm supposed to be intimidating her. My job is to get in, see what this female knows, and get her under control. Keep my pack safe. Easy. But now my wolf is all in a tizzy that we might be scaring her. Which is ridiculous. Since when does he care about a human's feelings more than the safety of the pack?

"I'd like this to be quick and painless, but it's up to you. Amber talked to you this afternoon. I need to know what she said."

She stares at me.

"This will go easier if you do as I say," I add.

Immediately, her back stiffens. "Did you just threaten me?"

"Miss—"

"Did you hurt Amber? Where is she?" She's on her feet now, voice rising to a shout. This five-foot-nothing pixie acts like she's going to challenge me. And my wolf... he thinks she's even cuter when she's mad.

"You better not have touched her, buddy," Foxfire hisses. "I told that moron Garrett, and I'm telling you. When it comes to Amber, *back off.*"

She is challenging me. She also called my alpha a moron. She either is crazy or suicidal.

"Miss Hines—"

"I meant it." She pokes me in the stomach, and my dominant side surges. I catch her wrist and pull her forward, turning her at the last minute so she ends up tucked against me, back to my front, my body bent over hers and nose buried in her rainbow-colored hair. I catch the scent of her: strawberry shampoo, printer ink, a bit of hippie incense, and a wild smell that hovers out of reach, familiar, but not something I can place.

She struggles, but she's trapped, a slender armful curved in all the right places. My dick takes this unfortunate moment to perk up.

"Let me tell you how this is going to go, sweetheart," I whisper in her ear. "I'm going to ask the questions. You're going to give me answers. And if you're very, very good, you and your friend will be fine. Understand?"

"Let me go." She rears up, stomping her feet on mine. Since mine are encased in biker boots and hers are bare, it probably hurts her more than it hurts me. I lift her off her feet and almost take a heel to my dick. I shift her to the side at the last moment, and her foot bounces off my thigh.

"Help, murder! Rape!" Foxfire shrieks. I clamp my hand over her mouth, and she bites me. My wolf decides he's in love.

In the next few seconds, we're down on the floor, my hand still over her mouth, my body weight pinning her. An interesting position for doing all sorts of things, my wolf points out. My dick agrees.

I flip her so she's facing me. Her chest rises and falls rapidly, and her scent's filled with fear, but her eyes spit fire.

"That's enough." I force enough dominance into my tone to cow a whole pack of wolves. "Are you going to cooperate, or do I have to tie you up?"

She makes a noise against my palm that sounds a lot like *fuck you.* I'm about to tell her I'd love to oblige when the doorbell rings. The goddamn pizza is here.

Maybe this isn't going to be so easy.

2

F *oxfire*

AS THE DOORBELL echoes through my house, the big guy pinning me to the floor shifts so he's holding most of his weight instead of smooshing me into the hardwood. Which is pretty considerate of him. I appreciate that sort of consideration, even in a man who burst into my house under the false pretense of pizza.

The doorbell rings again.

"Well?" My words come out muffled under his hand. "Are you going to get that?"

He moves his hand. "Are you going to behave?"

I lick my lips, and his gaze snaps to my mouth. He moves again, and suddenly I'm very aware of his impressive manhood pressed against my foxy bits. He's a big boy. Very big.

Oh my god, are we having a moment? I stare up at him. Strong jaw, firm lips. Heavily muscled body pressed to mine.

My tongue darts out to lick my lips, and his eyes follow every move. The weapon in his pants jumps against my leg.

I try to wriggle out from under him, and his grip tightens, reminding me that he's a foot taller and a helluva lot stronger than I am. I could scream, but that might put the delivery man in jeopardy. And I'm pretty sure it would make Mr. Wrestling Champ mad. The result: bad things. For me, for the delivery man, probably for Amber. And I won't get pizza.

For some reason, I'm not afraid of him. He smells...right. When it comes to people, I tend to trust my sense of smell. As weird as that sounds, it works.

Besides, I'm Foxfire Hines. I'm not afraid of anything, except toilet snakes.

The doorbell chimes again.

"I'll behave," I say, "if you pay for the pizza. But only because I care about Amber. And I'm hungry."

"You mean it?"

"Pinky swear?" He's pinned my wrists to the floor by my head, but I still can wriggle my baby finger.

The dude studies me a moment. I smile all sweet and innocent. Trustworthy.

He sighs and rises. "No funny business." He points a warning finger at me. "I'm not here to hurt you, but if you cause trouble, I will punish you."

My foxy bits quiver. I'm not turned on, no way. My nipples tent my top because it's cold. I wrap my arms around myself, just in case.

My giant unwanted guest is at the door, exchanging bills for a white-and-red square box. Not screaming was the right call. The delivery man isn't nearly as big and tall and hasn't hit the gym in a while. Mr. Muscles looks like he lives in one and sleeps on a bench press machine in-between reps.

"Don't forget the tip," I call.

A scowl, and my unwanted guest angles away from me. Yowza. The back is just as tight as the front.

I must have zoned out a little perving on the guy because the next thing I know, he's coming back toward me, pizza box in one hand, catching my elbow and propelling me to the couch with the other.

"Sit," he orders, and I do. As soon as my butt hits the couch, I reach for the pizza.

"Not so fast. First, we talk."

"This is cruel and unusual punishment," I blurt.

He gives me another *what the hell?* look, which I easily ignore. I get those a lot.

"Well, it is unusual. And cruel. I'm hungry."

"I'm gonna feed you. I need to ask you some questions first." He puts the pizza in front of me on the coffee table and props his boot on the edge between me and the object of my desire. Of course, this gives me a full on view of his crotch, displaying another potential object of my desire.

No! Bad Foxfire!

"Your friend's been talking about us. I'm here to see how much you know."

"Us? Who's us?" Reluctantly, I raise my eyes to his face. Now that I think of it, he does look familiar. Another neighbor of Amber's? Garrett's whole gang seems to live in the apartment building he owns. "I don't even know your name."

"It's Tank."

Tank. I don't question the weird name. Pot, kettle and all that. Besides, don't gang members all get badass nicknames when they go through initiation? I'd ask him, but I doubt he's up to fielding questions about gang life. And since he's built like, well, a tank, I'm going to let him get his way.

For now.

"All right, Mr. Tank—"

"Just Tank."

"Just Tank," I correct, and he closes his eyes in frustration. Excellent. "What do you want to know?"

He takes a deep breath. "Earlier today, you confronted Garrett outside Amber's apartment. You accused him of being a werewolf."

"Yeah? So?"

"I need to know what she told you about us."

"She didn't tell me anything. We were talking about her bad date. You guys were just mentioned in passing."

"What exactly did she say?"

"I can't tell you that. It would break the girl code."

"Miss Hines," he growls.

"Call me Foxfire."

"Miss Hines." His voice gets even more deep and growly. "I don't think you understand how serious this is. Amber learned some things about us and was sworn into confidence by our leader, Garrett. Because she talked, she could be in trouble."

"I thought you said she was okay?"

"We don't like outsiders talking about us. Her level of punishment depends on how much she told."

There was that word again. *Punishment.* I love it a little too much.

"You motorcycle types are pretty intense." I don't call them a *gang* because maybe that's offensive. Or maybe it isn't because they definitely are a gang. A bunch of big, dangerous guys covered in matching tattoos, riding motorcycles, sticking close together, and following some sort of bro code. Their leader owns a bunch of businesses, and they all work for him. I haven't heard a whiff of criminal activity, but I'm not going to ask.

"Just tell me what Amber told you."

The jingling of little bells interrupts us.

"Is this your phone?" Tank picks it up before I nod. He closes his fist around it and squeezes. When he opens his hand, pieces of cell phone fall to the floor.

"Whoa," I breathe, staring at the pieces.

"You need to start paying attention, Miss Hines. I'm here to find out what you know, and neither of us is going anywhere until I'm satisfied."

~.~

Tank

"THAT WAS SO COOL!" she squeaks. "You crushed my phone with your bare hands." She stops and wrinkles her nose. "Wait... that was my phone."

I can only shake my head. "Yeah, Princess. Until I get what I want, you're not going anywhere or talking to anyone."

"Can I have pizza?"

"Talk first. Then pizza."

"Amber didn't tell me anything about you guys."

"You called Garrett a werewolf."

"Yeah, because that's what you're called."

Fuck. I fold my arms over my chest. "Amber told you we were werewolves."

"Yeah."

"And you believed her?"

"Um, yeah. You're in a gang. It's your name. You can call yourself whatever you want, as far as I'm concerned. The Jets, the Sharks, the Werewolves... the Deranged Iguanas... whatever you think makes you badass, crew cut."

I swipe my fingers across my eyes. This chick has no idea how close she is to getting that cute little ass of hers spanked. And my dick thinks that's an *awesome* idea.

"So that's why you came down here?" she scoffs. "To ask me what I knew about your gang?"

"Tell me what you know."

"I know you ride motorcycles." She ticks off on her fingers. "A bunch of you live next to Amber, my best friend. Your leader tried to seduce her and failed, miserably, when he abandoned her halfway through their first date."

"Is that all?"

"A bunch of you have moon tattoos on your knuckles." She sneers. "Werewolf and full moon. Very original. You also own Club Eclipse. You stick to a theme, I'll give it to you. There." She throws her hands up in the air. "That's all I got. You came all this way to shake me down?"

"We don't like people digging into our private business."

"Well, I don't like jerks dating my friends. I don't care if Garrett the Wolfman owns half the property around here. He can't treat my friend that way."

I raise a brow. "Or what?"

She scoots forward and sticks a finger in my face. "I will end him."

I bite back a grin. She shakes the finger, and I mock snap

at it. She yanks her hand back with a yelp. Finally. A little fear.

"Very funny." She folds her arms across her chest, matching my own pose.

"Garrett would never hurt Amber."

"There are a lot of ways to get hurt," Foxfire says. "Only one of those is physical."

I incline my head. "You're right. I can see you're no threat to our organization. We don't want to cause trouble, but as you said, Garrett owns a lot of property, and he doesn't want someone spreading slander about him."

"Well, I'm sorry Garrett got his panties in a bunch. I didn't realize he was so sensitive."

Insulting my alpha again. If she were mine, she'd be over my knee so fast... hell, I'd be dizzy. I've never met someone so in need of a spanking in my life. "Watch it."

"You watch it." She glares at me.

Unbelievable. "You're five-foot nothing, and you think you can take me?"

"I'm five-five!"

"Yeah," I snort. "In five-inch heels." I don't know why I'm riling her up. My errand may as well be over. Garrett might want me to call a bloodsucker to mind-wipe her, but that can fuck up a person. I don't think she deserves that. Even if she has poor taste in hair dye.

"I can't believe you—you—"

"Careful." I can't believe I have to warn this chick off picking a fight with me. My wolf could eat her in one bite. Not that he would. I'm more interested in eating her a different way. After I warm her pretty ass.

Her face goes red.

"Sit down, Foxfire," I order.

She drops to the couch. *Very responsive.* The spunky attitude is all bluster—and who can blame her? She lives alone, her best friend is a workaholic stick-up-her-ass lawyer. It's Saturday night, and the Princess of La La Land is all alone.

"Obviously, we made a mistake." Garrett might not want to let her off this easily, but I'm not letting a bloodsucker touch her. We can find another way to keep her quiet. Not that she knows anything, but despite the smart mouth, she actually has a brain. If Garrett keeps sniffing around Amber, it might be only a matter of time that she realizes the truth.

"I gotta make a call. Eat your pizza." I flip the pizza box open and leave her to it, heading to a private corner to call my alpha. It rings a few times and goes to voicemail.

"Hey, Boss." I lower my voice. "I'm at the girl's place. She doesn't know anything. Thinks we're some sort of motor-cycle gang who call ourselves the Werewolves." I take a deep breath. I want to say I think we should leave her alone, but something stops my tongue. My wolf. He wants to hang around her more.

"I'll keep an eye on her until you call, see if I can get her to open up more."

I check my messages and texts, but there's nothing from the pack. I could try Trey and Jared, but at this point they had to be in Mexico, or close to it. I should be with them, going after our lost packmate, rather than babysitting Little Miss *Looney Tunes*. Now that I'm in her place, I smell mari-juana, although none of the stink is on her. She's not doing drugs. She's this whacked out on her own.

The sooner my alpha calls and orders me away from her, the better. My wolf doesn't agree, which makes it all the more true.

She's still sitting on the couch, watching me with wide eyes. The pizza lies untouched before her. "Where's Amber?"

"She's safe. Nothing's going to happen to her."

"How do I know you're not lying to me?"

"Behave, and I'll let you talk to her. Right now she's busy."

Foxfire glares at me.

"She's with Garrett."

"Garrett? That jackhole?"

I growl. "Don't insult him."

"He left my girl on the side of a mountain."

"He had his reasons." He was about go moon mad in public. "Amber was fine."

"Yeah, because I came and got her. If he seduces her again and breaks her heart, guess who's picking up the pieces? Me."

"Your girl is fine. She's totally safe. We thought she broke some rules, but Garrett is handling it."

"Rules? Geez, you guys are anal for a gang."

"You have no idea." I really want to give her a taste of who's boss between the two of us. But that's not part of the job. Too bad. Wolves discipline their mates. My wolf likes the idea of punishing her as much as my dick.

"Go ahead and eat." I motion to her.

She stares at me. "You're going to stay here?"

I nod.

"For how long?"

Until I know you're not a threat to the pack. "As long as I want to." She's breathing hard, her little shoulders rising and falling with anger. Her breasts stir under her shirt. The sight does interesting things to my cock. "You dye your hair?"

"No," she sneers. "It comes out this way naturally."

I can't help it. I laugh. She's too ridiculous.

I sit on the other end of the couch.

She stares at me like she's weighing the odds between cooperating and fighting back. For all I know, in a minute she might decide it's a good idea to try to push me off the couch.

I stretch out my legs. I'm six-three, 255 pounds of muscle. Plus, werewolf strength. In a wrestling match, I know who'll win. I almost hope she tries.

She comes to a decision and gives me a bright smile.

"Want some pizza?"

La La Land.

~.~

Foxfire

Tank blinks at me. He's pretty nice for a gang enforcer. Too big and muscly for his own good. Obviously not used to someone standing up to him.

He's in for a big surprise.

"I got supreme." I reach for a slice. "I figure I need to eat healthy, so I should get veggie, but then I crave meat. So I just get supreme and tell myself I'll pick off anything unhealthy. I hate olives, so I just pick them off. You're welcome to half."

"Okay," he says slowly.

"I didn't poison it," I say before taking a big bite. I chew, swallow, and grin. "You didn't give me enough time."

He freezes as he's reaching for the pizza. I smile wider, showing all my teeth.

I've decided to cooperate. In my own, fantastic Foxfire way. I'm going to act silly and clueless until he realizes his mistake. But I'm not letting him off easy. I'm going to make him pay. He's going to regret the day he messed with me. I'm going to drive him crazy.

In the meantime, pizza.

I polish off three pieces before I slow down. God, I was hungry. I've watched Tank the whole time. He looks familiar...

"I know where I saw you. You're the bouncer at Eclipse."

"And you're the chick who can't hold her liquor."

"I'm in the middle of a bad breakup. I'm allowed to overindulge." I gesture at him with my crust. "You'd better eat something, if you want any."

With a shake of his head, he reaches again for his first slice. He inhales it, reaches for a second, folds it onto a third slice to make a pizza sandwich, and eats it that way. Within minutes, he's decimated half the pie.

"Dude. Want me to order another?"

He shakes his head.

I study him further. Motorcycle boots, jeans, tee-stretched over his stunning Hercules physique. He carries the smell of motor oil, and something else—a scent like cinnamon spice, not unpleasant. I have a pretty good sense of smell. In the past, I've decided not to date guys or take on clients because they didn't smell right. Just another odd thing about me.

As big as he is, and as much as he's tried to intimidate me, he seems pretty reserved. His movements are careful, controlled. I can't see him hurting a woman. Maybe that's why I felt so comfortable pushing his buttons from the start.

"What?" he asks, and I realize I've been staring for over a minute.

"Nothing." I muster innocence.

"So how did you become a Werewolf?"

He almost chokes. "What?"

"I assume you weren't born riding a motorcycle. When did you join the gang?"

He clears his throat. "Not a gang. A club."

"Oh." I tilt my head to the side. "A club. Like the Mouseketeers?"

"No."

"Do you have a cheer?"

"No." He rubs his forehead.

"So, can women become Werewolves? I've always wanted to learn how to ride a motorcycle."

"We don't call ourselves that. At least not in public."

"Right. You just have moon tattoos and wolves painted on your bikes."

He glares at me, and I raise my hands in defense.

"What? You stick to a theme, like I said. I admire that. If you didn't want your name to be obvious, you shouldn't all hang out at Club Eclipse." Tank's expression is carefully blank, but I can see I'm getting to him. Good. "Does Garrett lead some sort of Monster Mash dance every full moon? 'Cause you should. In fact, that could be your initiation. A line dance to 'Thriller'."

He shakes his head.

"No? Then how do people join?"

"You can't join. You have to be sponsored."

"Who sponsored you?"

"My dad."

"He's in the club?"

"Yeah." He looks away, as if he didn't mean to give me that little tidbit.

"Oh, nice. A family affair." I smile sweetly, and his jaw clenches. He's practically grinding his teeth.

Excellent.

"So, if I get a motorcycle, would you be my sponsor?"

"No."

"No? I have a lot to offer a club. I can make a mean margarita. And margarita flavored cupcakes."

"No."

"I can fix the club's website. I've been there, and it is dire."

"You've been looking into us?"

Oops. He's all tense again, so I shrug. "Your little leader is dating my best friend. I did some digging." He glares, and I raise my hands. "Relax. Everything I found was legit. Except the website. A color scheme like that should be outlawed. Hey, if you let me go, I'll fix it for you at a friends and family discount."

"You do websites?"

"Yep. It's part of my business. Online marketing and branding. Here, I'll show you." I jump up. He rises, too, and I wave my hand. "I'm just getting my laptop."

"Don't take too long," he orders.

"I'm not going to escape out the window." Not yet anyway. Not if I can chase him off some other way. "How long did you say you were staying again?"

"As long as it takes."

"If you want something to drink, help yourself. I have water and water."

I grab my computer. Before I return, I stick my head into the bathroom and brush my teeth. I fluff my hair and apply some lip gloss. Not that I'm going to flirt or anything. But just in case. I give the girls a boost, you know, for support, not to show them off to a certain sexy biker.

When I return, he's cleared the pizza. And has a glass of water waiting for me next to his. He put both glasses on coasters.

"A housebroken werewolf," I murmur.

"Excuse me?" He glances up. He has sharp hearing. Good to know.

"You put the glasses on coasters." I smile at him. "Was your last girlfriend a bitch? Did she take you to obedience school?"

I chuckle at my own joke while Tank looks longingly at the door. Poor guy, stuck with me. I didn't go to college, but I've mastered the art of annoying people.

"Here." I open my laptop and show him my client portfolio.

"You did all this yourself?"

"Once you learn the basic design, it's not hard." I pull up my most recent projects and point out the before and after.

"It's good. Really, really good. You do great work."

"Well, thank you."

I sit back. Dammit, I need to stick to the plan. But impressing him feels too good.

I keep scrolling through my work. He leans close. Way close. The heat from his body seeps into me. His nose is practically in my hair, like he's—

"Dude, did you just sniff me?" I scoot away from him on the couch.

"Sorry," he mutters. "You smell…"

"I'm wearing deodorant."

"I know. I don't mean you smell bad. It's just…" he trails off with a frown.

"Just what?" I raise my arm and sniff, just to be sure. I didn't put on any perfume in the bathroom because I didn't want to be obvious.

"Nothing."

"Well, what about you? You smell like motor oil."

He blinks. "You smell that?"

"Yeah. I've always had a keen sense of smell. You work on cars or something?"

"Yeah. I run the shop."

"The shop? For the gang?"

"The club."

I pull up the club website and click over to the shop.

"You do good business?"

He shrugs.

I navigate around the site, ignoring him for a few minutes. This guy has me flustered in a way no other guy has before.

"You know, I'm not going to tell anyone about you guys. You can go now."

"Not until I hear from Garrett."

"You do everything he says?"

"He's a good leader." Tank stretches out his legs. "You got a TV?"

"No. TV rots the brain."

"And pot doesn't?"

"What?" I wrinkle my nose. "I don't do that anymore."

"Then what are those grow lights in the other room?"

"Those are for my tomatoes."

He just stares at me.

"Fine," I sigh. "We can watch Netflix on my computer."

3

F *oxfire*

THE NEXT THING I KNOW, Tank is closing my laptop.

"Bedtime."

"Wha—!" I cry. "It's only—" I glance at the clock. It's almost midnight.

"Come on." He points to the bedroom.

I yawn. I am pretty tired. "Okay, Big D."

He shakes his head but doesn't correct me. In fact, I think I see the corner of his lips twitch.

"Wait, are you spending the night?"

"You got it, Princess. Right out here." He's already found a blanket and pillow for the couch and brought in his black bag from his truck. He must've grabbed it when I was in the bathroom or something.

I pause a moment.

"You're not in any danger from me," he says quietly. For some reason, I believe him. Not sure why, but I do.

Still, the whole situation is stupid. House arrest over a misunderstanding.

As I brush my teeth in the bathroom, I consider my escape options. Maybe I could steal his phone and reach out to Amber. It's not Tank's presence that worries me so much as knowing Amber's caught up in some weird gang activity. My lawyer friend's idea of an exciting time is wearing yoga pants to brunch after her weekly Hatha class. Her hooking up with a wild tattooed motorcycle man neighbor is high on my list of *No way, never gonna happen.*

But I was rethinking that list. A few hours with Tank, and I'll never again underestimate the power that big, growly biker guys have on a lady's ovaries. I'm two shots away from climbing Tank like a tree.

I toss my rainbow-colored hair, squeeze my elbows together to push up my boobs, and pout at the mirror. "How do you like it, big man?"

"You okay in there?" Tank calls.

Crap. He must be right outside the door, making sure I don't climb out the window or something.

"Just a minute!"

I lick my lips and frown. There's another way to control a guy. I'm not ashamed—I've done it before, to get out of speeding tickets and the like. A little flirting hurts no one. And playing the annoying little sister isn't working.

I have to seduce him.

"Foxfire." Tank knocks a few minutes later. "Hurry up—"

I swing the door open before he finishes his sentence. "Oh, you're still here."

He blinks at me. In the past few minutes, crazy Foxfire

has become sexy Foxfire. I brushed and poofed my hair, added lip balm, spritzed some perfume. Nothing major.

Except now I'm naked under my bathrobe.

I wait until I'm in the bedroom before loosening the tie and letting it gape.

"It's too bad you have to stay here all night," I purr as he checks the windows. My house is old—someone painted the jambs shut thirty years ago. I won't be escaping that way.

If my seduction plan works, I won't need to.

Tank turns, takes one look at me, and stops. I smile at him.

"No," he practically growls. Is that alarm scrawling across his face?

I guess sex really is the best weapon. At least when dealing with a giant MC club enforcer. "What?" I bat my lashes.

He angles past me and goes to my dresser. He opens a drawer and rummages around.

"What are you doing?" I squawk, flying at him.

"Here." He thrusts a shirt at me. "Put this on."

"Why?"

"Because I told you to. And right now, what I say goes."

I pout. "But I sleep naked."

"Not tonight."

I shrug. "Fine." My bottom lip puffs out as I take the shirt. I wait until he meets my gaze. I shrug my shoulders, and the bathrobe falls to the floor, leaving me in nothing but my boy short panties.

His Adam's apple bobs, and I note his cock is swollen against his jeans. I've totally hit my target.

I shrug the shirt on, doing a little jiggle as I do and keeping my shoulders back. I don't often wear this tank top —it's tighter than I usually like. But tonight, it's the perfect choice. The lavender tank looks perfect with my skin, and my girls are on full display. "Is this what you wanted?"

The growl sounds again, deep in his chest. "Get in bed." His face is blank, but the tightness in his crotch hasn't lessened.

"Will you tuck me in?" I press forward, stomach fluttering with excitement.

"You don't want to do this."

"Do what, Daddy?" I'm close enough if I lean forward, my boobs will brush his chest. His rock-hard chest. Don't mind if I do.

As soon as my taut nipples touch him, electricity shoots from the tips to my foxy bits. Tingling spreads all through my lady parts, right into my core.

"No, baby." Tank grips my arms and sets me back a step, a strained look on his face. "This isn't what you want."

"I'm a big girl," I remind him. "I know what I want. Tonight, I want to be naughty."

"We can't," he says through gritted teeth.

His seriousness cuts through my aroused haze. "You don't want me?"

"It's not that." His big fingers close around a lock of my hair—a bright blue curl, carefully teased for his benefit. He squeezes, fist shaking, like an addict longing for a fix. Then he lets go. "You don't want to do this."

"Why not?"

"I'm rough." His hand collars my throat. He doesn't squeeze, just rests his fingers there, as if to demonstrate how dangerous he is.

I'm not put off. Not in the least. "Yeah?" I breathe.

"Yeah. When I fuck, I fuck hard." He pulls me forward and holds me against his chiseled body. I feel him. Every inch.

My pulse races.

"You wouldn't like it, baby. Because it's always going to be my way." He dips his head, and his lips touch my ear. "I say *spread*, and you spread. I say *ride*, and you ride." His whisper sends tingles through me. "I say *come*, and you come. And it's not over until I say it's over. Even if you beg me to stop."

Fireworks explode in my brain. My pussy squeezes as if he's already told me to come.

Benny was bad in bed. Really, really bad. So much so, I tended to encourage him to do his own thing, while I did mine. I'm essentially on a two-year dry streak.

My seduction plan just backfired. Big time.

"So what's it gonna be?" he murmurs, tucking a strand of hair behind my ear. "You gonna be my good girl?"

My lips part. "Yes," is on the tip of my tongue. My panties are soaked.

No, Foxfire! Bad, bad girl! I'm supposed to be seducing him, not melting into a puddle at his feet.

His lips drop to my ear. "You wanna be a good girl tonight, baby. You know why?"

"Why?"

"'Cause if you're bad... you get punished."

~.~

Tank

. . .

IT WAS SUPPOSED to be an easy job. Get in, handle the girl, get out. Protect the pack.

I'm leaning against the wall outside of Foxfire's bedroom with a boner the size of a baseball bat. I'm about to lose control. My wolf howls for its prey.

Foxfire. Fuck.

All evening, I alternated between wanting to dominate her and wanting to laugh. I've never met someone so annoying. And cute. And saucy. And smart. I want to punish her, smack that tempting ass, and spread her thighs. Find out how she sounds screaming *Daddy* when my tongue's working her clit. Get underneath all her games and teasing to find out what makes her tick. To be the one who makes her tick.

No. No messing with humans, even cute ones that fascinate my wolf.

I can almost hear my dad. He lectured me my whole life to beware the pussy trap. "Son, don't ever let a woman in. Give her an inch, she'll think she's a ruler."

I want to give Foxfire a lot more than an inch. But I don't want just to fuck her. I want to own her.

"Come on, come on," I mutter, jabbing the buttons on my cell phone. Garrett. Jared. Trey. None of them is answering calls or texts. I called Sam over at Eclipse, but the wolves working at Garrett's club tonight aren't as high up in the pack, and they know nothing. I don't tell them what's going down—Garrett doesn't want word getting out about his missing sister, Sedona. I'm his second. I have his back. I just wish he'd call.

Scratch that. I wish I could fuck Foxfire into next week, then get my alpha's call.

"Pack comes first," my dad told me. "Always. A mate can trick you, a woman will leave you, but the pack will never let you down. Everything we have, we owe to our fellow wolves."

"I'm trying," I mutter. For a second, I think about calling my dad, but no. He's in another pack, and I know what he'll say. I'm not in the mood for a lecture.

This is my problem, and I'm going to face it like a grown man. I'm going to wait until Foxfire's asleep and then jack off a couple of times. Hopefully, that will relieve the tension until morning, when I see her again. I don't even mind the freakish hair. It's got me wondering—if those are the curtains, what color are the drapes?

One thing at a fucking time.

I pocket my phone—carefully, not a lot of extra room in my jeans anymore—and start to tiptoe away when I hear it.

Scrape, scrape, scrape.

What the fuck?

I open the door.

Foxfire shoots me a guilty look from the window. She's got a metal nail file and is trying to work open the paint-sealed window.

"What are you doing?"

"Trying to get some fresh air?" She hides the tool behind her back.

I want to laugh because she's the cutest fucking prisoner I've ever seen, but instead I keep my face blank. I can't let her know her antics are working.

And believe me, I do know she's working me with them.

"Nice try, Princess." I clamp a hand on the back of her neck, ignoring the way her pulse jumps under my palm.

A scent fills the air, and I get a lungful as I guide her to the bed. Hot, fresh pussy.

"Get in, little girl." I pull the blankets down.

"Read me a story?" she mocks with a hopeful little-girl face.

"I'm not your father."

She hangs one finger from her mouth, the perfect coquette. "I know, big man." Her bottom points in my direction as she climbs up, and I can't help it. I smack her sassy ass.

She squeaks.

"That didn't even hurt." Not over her boy shorts. I grab her hips and nip the offended flesh, then kiss it better.

She goes still, breath hitching.

Fuck. What am I doing? I definitely have zero intention of getting involved with this crazy human, no matter how cute she may be.

I slap her ass again. It's addictive how good her soft flesh feels under my hand.

"Get in that bed before I peel these panties down and give you a proper spanking," I growl.

I'm not sure if I meant that to be a threat or an enticement, but she clearly isn't scared.

I somehow wrangle my self-control and take a step back so she's out of reaching distance.

"Get in and scoot over."

She obeys. I can't tell if I'm relieved or disappointed. "What are you doing?"

I grab a pillow—she's got about a million, all different shapes and sizes. A few of them spill onto the floor as the bed sags under my weight. Tight fit, but we'll make it work. "I'm going to sleep."

"With me?"

Hell, yes, with you! my wolf asserts.

Down, boy.

I try for stern. "If you're lucky, all I'll do is sleep." I lie down, my big body caging her against the wall. "Keep up the games, and I'll punish you for real. Then we'll sleep." I swear I scent her arousal, which makes my cock surge into ready mode.

"Whatever you say, big man," she says sweetly, and I'm pretty sure she's won this round because I'm the asshole with a hard-on so thick it could lift a car, and all she has is my handprint on her ass.

"Good girl," I rumble. *That's right, sweetheart. You're not the only one who can play that game.*

I've started to relax when a small voice asks, "What exactly do you mean by punish me?"

"Keep pushing, and you'll find out." I drape my arm over my face, but it's no use. I'm sprung. I should've taken the floor.

A deep breath is my only warning before Foxfire makes her next move.

My dick is suddenly happy—very happy—to be straddled by a lithe little body. Her hands rest on my pecs, and she leans forward, her breath warming my face.

In one move, I roll and pin her. Her breath shudders out of her, and the scent of her arousal *definitely* fills the air.

"Tank?"

"You *don't* want this, baby." Seriously. I would tear her apart. Her hips jerk, and I thrust my erection into the notch between her legs.

Oh fuck, I think she's wet for me. Even through my jeans, I can feel her panties are hot and damp. She wraps her slender legs around my waist, inviting me home.

I shove her tight tank top up and groan at the sight of her breasts. Not too big, not too small. A perfect handful. "Oh baby, those nipples were meant to be licked, weren't they?"

She arches up, offering them to me. I lean over and flick one with my tongue, then graze it with my teeth.

When I look back up at her face, her gray eyes are wide. All pretense is gone. She's not playing crazy or babygirl, she's panting and watching me, apparently transfixed.

I slam my hips home again, wishing like hell I wasn't just dry humping this little beauty.

She gasps. "Ow—um, you're hurting me."

Instantly, I let go and jerk away.

Fuck.

"No, it's okay," she says. It was just my hair was caught under the weight of your hand."

No, I would definitely hurt her if I kept going. Better to stop now before I've gone so far, it's not possible. I scrub my face, angling away from her so she doesn't see how very close I am to tearing her skimpy clothes off and finishing what she started.

"Stay here. Go to sleep," I say.

~.~

Foxfire

I'm all hot and bothered. I could finger myself, but Tank's so close, he might hear me. He has really good hearing. And a good sense of smell. And he can practically see in the dark.

Too bad he's not gonna fuck me. He must have some sort of code of honor, because I know he wants me. I never thought of motorcycle men as prudes, but there ya go.

Now I wish I hadn't said he was hurting me. I meant for him to move his hand from my hair, not to jump off me like I burned him.

I wait a few minutes and then pad out of the bedroom, heading for the kitchen. If I can't seduce him, I'll escape another way.

"Foxfire? What are you doing?"

"Just getting a drink of water."

If you're not back in bed in two minutes—"

"I know, I know, punishment," I call back merrily and turn on the water, but not before I hear a creak. He's coming into the kitchen. It's now or never.

I duck into the little room off the kitchen and crouch by the door. For once, I'm glad Benny didn't get around to replacing it. It came with a doggie door—useless because I've never had a pet. Useless, until now.

"What the fuck?" Tank growls just as I scramble through the flap.

"Stop," he shouts. He comes after me, hitting the door, but the deck is warped, and the door only opens partway. Another Benny project, never finished, the lazy asshole. The door opens enough that I can slip through, but a guy built like a Tank won't have so much luck.

Then Tank hits it again, with such force it shudders but doesn't break. Damn. Tough guy.

I find my feet and run, glad I thought to put on sneakers. I race up the small hill behind my house and down into the wash.

I chose this house because it was cute, right near downtown, but with the back yard against a wash, which means I get front row access to wildlife and desert. The nearby open space relaxes me. When it's nice, I work out on the patio, looking over the sandy banks, tangled with mesquite and creosote. I imagine running out there, hiking all day to find out where it ends, getting lost and found again in the wild.

I never thought I'd need a place to run and hide.

I bound into the wildness, my sneakers scrabbling on the rocks.

"Get back here," Tank roars. He'd better keep quiet if he doesn't want the neighbors waking up.

I would make for a nearby house and bang on their doors, but it's the middle of the night. There's no telling how long it'll take for them to answer. Not to mention, they might be just as annoyed at me as at Tank. I have a bit of a reputation as the resident weirdo.

My best chance is to lose Tank in the wild out here and hide. I dart around a cactus and crouch.

Tank runs fast for such a big guy. And quiet.

Folded in half, I sprint again. The moon lights my way, and I've always had pretty good night vision. But Tank does, too.

After my fourth sprint, I hide behind a boulder and wait. I listen, but there's no sound.

My skin prickles. There's something out there, breathing heavily. Instincts older than time tell me it's not human.

Something's out here, and it's hunting me.

I peer around the boulder and meet glowing eyes. My stalker is some sort of giant black dog. A pet off its leash? Or something more sinister?

Tank's name is on my lips. The man I'm trying to escape is the one who can save me. Ironic, but there it is.

I spring up from my crouch and run hard.

Behind me, the beast snaps into motion. I'm running as fast as I can, and it's gaining on me. "Help," I scream. "Help, Tank, help!"

A growl rings out behind me. It's close. I'm going to die in the brush, torn apart by a wild animal.

And then—

Everything changes.

The darkness sharpens, and suddenly I see everything. Scents burst in my nose—the fresh-rain smell of creosote, the distant bloom of citrus trees. Something in the bush twitches—a feathery body, hiding and praying the predators will pass. I smell its fear.

The moon shines her spotlight on me. My head whips back. My spine crackles. My body shrinks... my hands morph from five-digit human ones to furry paws. I land hard on all fours, my body aching, my nose twitching with a thousand new smells. I'm tangled in layers of fabric. Yipping, I claw my way out of the tent of my old clothes. My legs scrabble against the sandy earth as I break free. I shake hard, and the tingles on my skin fade. My fur stands on end. My tail fluffs up like a pissed off cat's. My long body feels sleek and strong.

Fur? Tail? Wait a minute.

I point my nose to the moon and yip. My four paws stay solid on the ground.

Paws? Now I'm really starting to freak.

There's something I'm forgetting. Something I'm supposed to be doing.

A growl ripples over the grass to my left. A dark shape crouches there, eyes glowing.

What was I doing? ...oh, yes. *Running for my life.*

With a high-pitched bark, I leap forward and race through the underbrush. There's a puddle ahead. If I roll in it, I might diffuse my scent. The wolf behind me won't be able to track me so easily.

Wolf? Now, how do I know that?

Teeth snap at my heels. My body finds new speed—the energy of the hunted. I surge forward. My four paws strike the ground seamlessly.

Paws? Four? What?

As soon as I think about it, I lose the rhythm.

One leg misfires, and I go flying. I flop on my side, feet waving in the air in a desperate scramble to get back up.

A shadow falls over me, and a growl makes me freeze.

The wolf stands over me, lowers its head, and sniffs along my white belly. My paws shake in the air.

The beast... transforms. Moonlight shimmers as the black fur sucks away, revealing tattooed skin and bulging muscles. Tank stands over me in human form.

"Foxfire?" His voice is growly rough, like a wolf's. My heart's gonna explode.

"Change back," Tank orders.

A sudden pressing urge comes over me, like a sneeze. I succumb to it, and my body takes human shape. I shout, convulsing with surprise.

"Foxfire, it's okay. You're okay." Tank kneels beside me, holding my shoulders, steadying my thrashing body. My limbs tingle like they've been asleep, but other than that, it doesn't hurt. Not like my head, which is spinning. And—oh fuck—I'm naked.

"Wha—" I sputter. "What the hell just happened?"

~.~

Tank

. . .

She's a fox. An actual fox, with white-tufted tail and rust-colored fur. Narrow nose and perky ears. She's similar enough to a wolf that I caught the scent on her but didn't know what it was until she shifted. An actual fox shifter. I've never seen one before. I didn't know they existed until she transformed before my eyes and ran away, beautiful and lithe in the moonlight.

This... complicates things.

I scoop her up and carry her back up the wash. She whimpers in my arms. Her body trembles, and tears glint on her lashes. She's scared as hell. Of me? Or of the shift? I somehow got the feeling this was her first time.

"Breathe, baby, breathe," I murmur.

We're both naked, but that's not why she's shivering.

"I'm losing my mind. The moonlight, it called to me. And I..." She raises her hands and stares at them in horror. "I had paws!" She turns wide eyes on me. "And you were a wolf!"

Yep. First time.

"Okay, baby. It's going to be okay." I kicked the door open. I half-broke it before I decided to just change into a wolf and go through the doggie door. My clothes are in a pile on the old linoleum, but I don't stop.

"Please tell me this was a bad trip," she whimpers. "We did mushrooms or acid or something, and it's just a dream —it's just a dream."

"Shhh." I head to the couch, set her down, and pull a blanket around her. "Stay." I put alpha compulsion into my voice. It seemed to work before, getting her to shift back. Thank the moon for that. Otherwise, she could be stuck in fox form a long time, trying to figure it out.

Some shifters shift naturally. Others need the supervision of an alpha. Most of us have the benefit of the pack and plenty of experienced shifters to walk us through it. At least wolves do. We're pack animals.

Foxes—I'm not so sure. As far as I know, the little lady freaking out on the couch is the only one. Of course, small, weaker shifters don't often make themselves known. If wolf packs are secretive, fox dens, if they exist, probably hide like their lives depend on it.

I grab an energy drink out of my things and a bag of beef jerky.

"Here. Drink this." I hold the bottle for her. She's shaking but reaches for the beef jerky on her own. "You expended a lot of energy, running from me and shifting twice. You always need to eat and drink enough afterward, or it could be dangerous."

"I-I've never done that before."

"I know, baby." I tug on a pair of workout shorts, glad I brought a couple of changes of clothes. Of course, I expected to be done with this job in a few hours, tops, and then be on my way to Mexico.

The pale, rainbow-haired beauty trembles on the couch, and my wolf will be damned if he'll leave her now.

Things just got a lot more complicated.

4

F *oxfire*

Fuck. Fuck. Fuck.

This is a dream. A really bad dream, like the time Sunny left her mushrooms out and I ate them and thought the walls were melting.

The clarity of the moonlight, the scents that surrounded me, they were beautiful, but it's way worse than a bad trip.

"Here." Tank sits down next to me, holding out a power bar.

"No more jerky?" I ask hopefully.

"Carnivore?"

"I tried to be vegetarian, like, so many times. I would have these cravings where I almost ate raw meat."

"She wouldn't let you."

"Who?"

"Your fox. She's pretty, by the way."

"My…"

"Your fox. That's who came out to play just now. She's gorgeous."

I stare at him, remembering the harmony in my limbs, when I didn't think about it, the freedom, the whole new world of scents, beautiful and profane.

"What am I?"

"You really don't know?"

"Um, no. One minute I'm… on two legs and then the next I'm…" My breath gets stuck in my throat. "I'm—"

"Okay, okay, relax." He rubs my back. "Just breathe. It'll be okay. You're a shifter, like me. Most of us have the benefit of growing up in a house surrounded by shifters. My dad coached me through my first change. I was early. Some kids don't shift until their teens and then wake in bed all furry. It usually happens in adolescence, if not before."

"It's never happened to me."

"Yes, well, if I had to guess, I'd say your fox is shy. And she's on her own, without family or protection."

I lean into him. My heart isn't pounding as hard, but Tank is the only one keeping me on Earth.

Foxes. I'm a fox.

"You're a shifter," I state.

"Yeah, baby. I'm a wolf."

I let out a noise, half laugh, half gurgle. "I noticed."

He rubs my back some more.

"So that's why Garrett sent you. You're not part of a gang called the Werewolves. You are a werewolf."

"A pack," he says after a long silence. "I'm part of a pack."

"With Garrett?"

"Yeah."

No wonder they're secretive. I'd be less surprised if I

found the path to another world in my closet, but it actually reassures me. At least Garrett and Tank's behavior makes more sense now.

I open my hands, close them. Hands, not paws. No claws. Not right now.

"Are there others like me?"

"Not that I know of."

"Oh." Again, the world tilts under my feet.

"Foxfire... is there anyone... Do you know anyone in your family who might... have a secret?"

"What, like my great aunt Agatha's chili recipe? Oh, and she turns into a Saint Bernard during the full moon?"

Tank just looks at me, forehead wrinkled. He must think I'm really losing it.

"No." My breath shudders out of me. "Nothing like that. I don't really have a family—only my mom. And I don't think she'd hide something like this from me." I rub my hands. Hands. Not paws. No fur. "I'm cold."

He grabs the blanket and tucks it tight around me, wrapping an arm around my shoulders and giving me a side hug. "It's the shift. It takes energy. And you're skin and bones."

"I am not." I frown at him.

"You are, baby." He squeezes me tight, pulling me closer. "Petite."

"Yes, well, I was born this way. Not all of us can be freakishly tall and built like a truck."

"A tank."

"Yeah." Something he said unravels. "Wait, so you think someone else in my family is a shifter?"

"Shifters breed shifters. It's genetic."

"So my mom or dad..."

"One of them carries the gene. Most likely they can shift.

It'd be almost impossible for two non-shifters with the dormant gene to bear one who can shift."

"My mom." I shake my head. "I don't think she's a shifter. I lived with her. I've known her all my life."

"She never snuck off into the wilderness for hours at a time?"

"No. She does a lot of pot, but that's about it."

Another long silence. "What about your dad?"

"I don't know him."

Tank nods.

I swallow. I never met my dad. Around first grade, I decided I wanted to, but that was only because we were doing a class project on our parents. Mom helped me do half the project on her, and half on the host of my favorite show, *Reading Rainbow*. My entire class ending up thinking I was LeVar Burton's daughter. My popularity went way up, and I haven't given a thought to my mystery sperm donor since.

Except, now. Because of him, I turn into a fox. The thing that will most impact my life, given by a man I've never met.

I sigh.

"It's okay, Foxfire," Tank says again and squeezes me tight. He may be a giant, grouchy lump most of the time, but he's pretty good at reassuring me. I feel a lot better in his arms anyway. If he wasn't here, I'd be a complete mess. Probably ready to commit myself to the loony bin. "It's going to be all right."

"How is it all right? I turn into an animal during the full moon."

"Not just then. With practice, you'll be able to shift at will."

"Oh, goody. I can wow them at dinner parties."

A sound rumbles in his chest—a half-growl. "No. No dinner parties. You have to keep this a secret."

"No shit, Sherlock."

He catches my chin lightly. "Okay, baby. First rule of any pack. You give animals bigger and deadlier than you your respect. I'm telling you now so you don't get it beaten into you by someone less sympathetic than I am."

I try to think of something snarky as his dominant gaze bores into me. "Fine," I mumble, dropping my eyes.

"Good girl." He tucks me closer. I'm practically on his lap. He nuzzles my hair. He's sniffing me again. This time, I don't mind. Must be a wolf thing.

"So, does this mean I'm one of your pack?"

"No," he says quickly.

I hide my flinch. This creature, this animal inside me, she wants her kind.

"Most shifters keep to their own. But I've never heard of a pack of fox shifters. You're the first one I've seen."

Great. I'm still a freak, no matter what species. Whatever.

I sit up and scoot away from him to shake out my hair. It's a mess, full of sticks and grass. I comb my fingers through it.

"Let me," Tank murmurs and picks out the rest. When he's done, he keeps his arm around me.

"Thanks." Slowly, I let myself relax. "What now?"

"Now, we wait. You need rest. In the morning, I feed you."

"You're staying?"

"You're still my prisoner. And we both know I can catch you, no matter how far you run."

I nod. I'm too tired to argue. He's been here only a few

hours, and he's already a fixture in my life. But I'm glad. I feel safer with him, somehow.

I'm a fox. Fuck. I tuck my face into his shoulder. He's so big and so strong. And when I... my fox came out, he knew just what to do. I'm too tired to think about what that means, but maybe, for just tonight, I don't have to.

"I always knew I was different," I mumble.

"What's that, baby?"

"My mom. She's weird. And she raised me."

"Did she ever leave for periods of time or act strange around the full moon?"

"She's my mom. She was always strange." I remember kids pointing at us. Laughing. My name, my petite body, my hippie mom, smelling of patchouli oil and dressing us in clothes from Goodwill. Weird.

I realize I said all this out loud when Tank tightens his hold on me.

"It's going to be okay."

I wrap my arms around him and bury my face in his chest. He cups the back of my head as he murmurs, "We'll figure it out, together."

5

F *oxfire*

I DREAM of my paws scrabbling in the rocky earth. A sunset blazes in the distance, fiery red and orange. My broken cell phone crackles with my mother's voice, telling me I should dye my hair those colors. Then Tank looms over me, shaking his head...

I wake with a start, the smell of bacon so intense, I can taste it.

My stomach rumbles as I pad to the kitchen. Tank stands at the stove, his broad back hunched and shaved head bowed over a skillet.

"OMG," I say. "Are you making breakfast?" A folded paper bag soaks up grease under a stack of bacon. "Is some of this for me?"

He flashes me a grin, jerks his head at the table. My little card table is covered with dishes of meat. Sausage, hamburger patties, more bacon.

"Oh my god, Tank. Did you kill every pig and cow in the world?"

"Just for you, baby. Eat up."

Baby. I like that.

Bad Foxfire!

"I'm such a bad vegan," I mumble as I sit down.

"Seriously?" Tank raises a brow.

"What? I thought it'd be healthy."

"You can't be vegan."

"Why not?"

"'Cause you're a carnivore." Tank puts a plate of bacon right in front of me.

"I could eat tofu and stuff," I argue, as if I'm not about to swallow a pound of delicious pig.

"You can't cut meat out. Your fox won't let you."

Right.

That.

My stomach twists.

"Eat, baby." Tank gets more bacon going, then comes to the table. "You had a long run last night. Your fox needs this." His hand settles on the back of my neck, calming the storm in my stomach. I nod and pick up a strip of bacon. In no time, I've demolished half the plate, and a third of the sausages. Just enough to take the edge off my hunger. I've always had a great metabolism. Guess now I know why.

Tank moves around my kitchen as if he owns it. He's so big, but somehow he fits.

"I had a dream about my mom last night," I announce. Tank doesn't look up from the stove, but I know he's listening. "Do you think she knew?"

"She did name you Foxfire."

"That could just be her. Trippy hippy. She smoked pot all through her pregnancy."

"That explains a lot," Tank mutters.

"Hey!" I pout in his general direction.

He comes with a fresh round of meat and spills half of it on my plate before bumping my foot with his in a silent order. We chew for a while.

"Do you remember ever shifting before?"

I put down my fork and think. "I once ate some mushrooms and felt like I had fur. You didn't happen to give me any mushrooms last night...?"

He shakes his head as he goes back to the skillet.

"Didn't think so." Too much to hope for.

~.~

Tank

SHE'S STEWING AGAIN, frowning at the window. I dreamed of her last night, running and catching her and pulling her into position under me. I shift in my seat, glad the table doesn't have a glass top. I've got to get myself under control.

I clear my throat. "There are benefits to being a shifter."

"Yeah?"

"Yeah. Being able to eat this much, for one. You'll need to bring extra food with you when you go to shift."

"Where would I go? Wouldn't I just run out here?" She nods to the wash.

"In an pinch, yes. But be careful. People around here like to shoot coyotes, even though it's illegal. In the dark, your fox could be mistaken for a small one."

"All right." Her forehead wrinkles.

"You have to let your fox out once in a while. Once a month at least. Otherwise... well, it might be different than for wolves. But it helps you maintain balance." My voice holds an echo of my father's words, teaching me our way of life at the kitchen table. "It's important to take care of your animal. Feed her meat, let her out to run."

"It's like I'm a dog."

"You are. A wild dog."

"So you... run regularly? Where?"

"The Catalina mountains. But also A Mountain, in a pinch." A Mountain is the small peak near downtown painted with a large letter A for the University of Arizona. It's where Garrett shifted and ran off on his date with Amber the day before yesterday.

I bite back my offer to have her come on a moon run with the pack. "You might be able to get away with some midnight runs out along this wash. But a better choice is a wildlife preserve, somewhere that bans hunters. Even then, you have to be careful." I cut myself off before I scare her. But I'm worried. Poachers, other animals, shifters, anyone who sees a pretty fox and decides they want her. Especially another wolf. My wolf is rabid at the thought of another male sniffing around her.

I stand and clear the breakfast dishes. Foxfire stays zoned out. Maybe she's in a meat coma. She's never sat so still for so long.

My wolf insists we go and comfort her. But it's better she doesn't come to rely on me too much. She needs her own kind. A fox den, maybe a mate.

My fingers curl into the countertop. I release it before I leave an imprint.

Not a mate, my wolf growls. *Not anyone but me.*

I check my phone. No messages. Something's wrong. But Garrett told me to watch Foxfire, so that's what I'm going to do. Even if I now have my own reasons.

My dad wouldn't approve. But who else is going to take care of her?

I approach the table, and Foxfire startles. Her big eyes snap to mine. Wide, dreamy. Sweet face, *Loony Tunes* hair. She's so small and, deep down, submissive. No wonder her fox stayed dormant for so many years.

"Come on," I rap the table in front of her. She jumps but doesn't move. "Time to get up. Face the day."

"Are we going somewhere?" She arches an eyebrow.

"You need to act normal. Do whatever you do on a Sunday."

"Normally, I'm not under house arrest."

The bluster, it's an act. She's too smart for her own good. And she's been alone too long, without anyone to watch out for her.

My wolf wants to give her everything she needs.

"I guess I'll take a shower." She scoots out of her chair. "Maybe then I'll feel normal. Human."

She pushes past me, and I ignore her disrespect. She's acting out because she's scared. And I'm not her pack leader.

I grew up knowing I was a shifter. Expecting it. Meeting my wolf was a beautiful thing, a rite of passage. I felt powerful.

Foxfire emerges from the bathroom, clean and glowing. Her hair falls in soft rings around her pixie-like face. She struts out in cut-off shorts and a tight top, cleavage popping.

"Oh no." I stand. "You need to change."

"Why?" she shoots back, pretending to be oblivious to her body's effect on me. "We're staying here all day, right?"

"Just... put on some clothes." I don't need the temptation.

She puts her hands on her hips. "What's your problem with these?"

I grit my teeth. My problem is, my dick is hard enough to punch through a door. I'd send her to her room for the day, but I don't trust myself.

"Just change."

"Sure." She shrugs and strips off her shirt. It falls to the floor between us.

"Foxfire," I growl.

"You want me to change, Daddy Pops? I'm changing." She shoots me a lethal smile. Sweet as strychnine.

"Don't push me, baby," I growl. "I warned you what would happen."

"Mmm." She twirls a rainbow curl around one finger. "You've made a lot of threats. I have yet to see you carry through with any of them."

Fates help us both. She has no idea what I want to do with that hot little body of hers. And it starts with showing her who's boss. In more ways than one.

"Okay, baby. Let's do this." I lean down and pick up her shirt and toss it at her. "Bedroom, now."

She smirks and waltzes in that direction.

I fully planned on insisting she get dressed and having a sit-down discussion about dominant animals and her required submission.

Instead, I snag her wrist and spin her to face the wall. I press her small hand beneath mine against the textured plaster, pick up the other, and add it to my collection. She's still topless, and now I have the world's best top view of her cleavage. *Heaving* cleavage. Because she's definitely excited by my little show of who's boss.

I pin both her wrists against the wall with one hand and squeeze her breast roughly with the other. My open mouth finds the column of her neck. "You need to understand something, little fox. In a pack, there are rules."

"I thought you said I wasn't pack?" There's a hurt quality to her voice that makes my wolf whine.

"Shifters, then. Either way, you need to know the limits on your behavior."

"If I misbehave, I'll get groped by a hot wolf?" she suggests hopefully.

I suppress a laugh. "I mean it. Following the rules can save your life." She doesn't understand how dangerous this world is, and that's the part that has my wolf going nuts.

"Okay."

I release her breast and rest my palm on her ass. "Your actions have consequences. Shifters who step out of line are punished."

"You gonna ground me?" Her voice is pure sex, husky.

"Mm, no," I rumble in her ear. I work the button on her short-shorts with my free hand and tug them until they drop to the floor. "I take a more hands-on approach."

She waggles her ass in a clear invitation.

Fates, I want to take this so much farther than I'm going to. I have images flashing in my brain of stripping her completely naked and pounding her hard from behind.

Instead, I bring my palm down on her panty-clad ass.

"Ooh!" She jumps.

Did I spank her too hard?

I crane my neck to see her face. She's biting her lip, cheeks flushed with color, eyes glazed.

She likes it.

I smack her cute ass again. And again.

And then the goddamn doorbell rings.

~.~

FOXFIRE

TANK GOES RIGID. He releases me in a flash and yanks my top over my head. Motioning for me to stay put, he heads to the door.

So, of course, I yank on my jean shorts and follow him. He stops in the hall.

"It's a man," he says softly. "I can smell him."

I wrinkle my nose. I can't smell anything that specific yet. "It's probably Benny. He's supposed to come by to get his stuff."

He catches my arm. "Are you going to be cool?"

I roll my eyes. "Don't worry. I'm not going to run now. You're the only one telling me I'm not crazy."

"I wouldn't go that far."

"Har har. I'll be right back. Stay out of sight." I wave Tank into the kitchen, and he goes, face stony.

Should I flaunt my ex in front of him? He went nuts over my Daisy Dukes.

The doorbell goes again.

"Coming," I sing and open the door.

It's not Benny but a guy wearing a trench coat. It's still early on a Sunday morning, and my neighborhood is pretty quiet. We don't usually get solicitors.

"Can I help you?"

"Foxfire Hines?"

"That's me," I chirp. "Can I help you?"

"Yes." The man pulls his hand from his pocket and points a gun at me.

~.~

Tank

I SMELL the gun before Foxfire's fear hits me, bitter and potent. My wolf snarls.

I pad through her "grow light room." Maybe I can move fast enough to get to him before he sees what's coming.

My lips curl back. My wolf is ready to hunt.

"What the fuck is this about?" My rainbow-haired pixie puts her hands on her hips. I groan *No, Foxfire. Behave.*

"Just get inside, sweetheart. We'll talk it over."

"Who are you?" she demands. "Who sent you?"

What is it about her that makes her bluster in the face of danger? Now is not the fucking time. Does she think the gun is a toy?

I want to smack her ass all over again.

The man pushes inside, and she trips and falls with a soft cry.

I see red. Five seconds later, the thug is on the floor at my feet. I kick the gun away.

"Foxfire. Shut the door."

She scrambles to obey.

The man is unconscious. Considering how hard I hit

him, he'll probably be out for a while. He's lucky I didn't kill him. I still might.

I use a blanket to grab the gun, and then I wrench it open, emptying the chamber.

Unmarked. Street gun. Mine, now. My wolf snarls. I focus on the gun to keep my wolf from tearing the man apart.

"Duct tape in my bag," I tell her. She nods and rushes to get it. I tie the man and cover his mouth.

Foxfire is pale and trembling. I take a deep breath and get my rage under control. Ripping this man limb from limb won't solve anything and will terrify her.

"Come here." I open my arms. She dashes to them. Her body is so tiny. I swing her up and carry her to the couch, where I can comfort her and keep my eyes on the thug.

"What does he want?" Foxfire shudders.

"I don't know, baby," I nuzzle her throat. She's alive. She's safe. She's in my arms. Foxfire and her crazy hair. I use a fistful to tug her head back, gently, and take her mouth. She tastes like melon and strawberries, sugar and spice, and everything Foxfire.

My lips stroke over hers, despite the man unconscious on the floor. She's mine. Her nipples pebble against the thin shirt, and I'm about to lay her down and claim her. When I back off, she's got stars in her eyes. I put them there. My wolf is satisfied.

"You're going to be okay," I tell her.

She stares at me, wide-eyed. "What are we going to do with him?"

Normally, I'd make a few calls. But this job has morphed into something no one expected. "I'll figure it out. I'm going to make sure he's not a danger to us and try to get some answers. Can you go into your room and work for a while?"

"Yeah. Um, Tank? Can I use your phone, to check my messages?"

"Sure, baby."

Once she's gone, I kneel down next to the thug. He has the look of an ex-fighter, rough hands, beefy strength, belly gone a little soft. A local muscle-for-hire. Not too bright. He should've come with backup. But he was thinking he'd shake down a small, unarmed woman. He didn't expect me.

I step into kitchen for a moment while my wolf rages.

Foxfire. Fuck. She could've been killed. Or—

"Tank!"

I spin around as she hustles toward me. Something's wrong. Her face is even paler than it was. Her eyes wide and frantic.

"I think I know who he is. We need to go, now." She whirls and starts for the door. I catch her, holding her still when she struggles.

"Tell me, baby. What's wrong?"

She holds up my phone. "My mom called. She's in trouble."

~.~

Foxfire

"Listen to this." I jab the phone at Tank.

"Foxfire?" My mom's voice comes over speaker. "I just wanted to make sure you're okay. I'm in a bit of trouble and had to throw away my phone. There might be some men who come asking after me. Just tell them I'll get the payment when I can. Stay safe, sweetie."

Tank plays the message again while I bite my lip. "Sounds like she owes the wrong people money."

"No shit, Sherlock," I hiss. His face turns to stone, and I remember how wolves don't like to be challenged. Well, tough. This is my *mom* we're talking about. "She left me a message last night, but I didn't get it because you killed my phone. Dammit! This is your fault!"

He rubs his jaw. "I'm sorry for that. I really am. And I get you're mad, but dial back the challenge, baby, or my wolf will feel like he has to remind you who's in charge here."

The very recent memory of what form that reminder will come in rises up, a shimmering temptation. But now is not the time. "Whatever." I fold my arms over my chest.

Yeah, he just gave me the best kiss of my life and punched out a gunman to save me.

Whatever. I'm still pissed.

"I need to go," I tell him.

"Go where?"

"Go help her! I need to fix this."

Tank looks from the thug lying at the floor to me. "And just how are you going to do that?"

"I'll figure it out."

He catches my arm. "You're not going anywhere, baby."

"Oh please. I'm hardly going to tell your little secret. I'm one of you, remember?"

"Hush." He pulls me into the kitchen. "You need to be quiet about that."

"Well, I am. One of your little gang now, right? The furries?"

"You can't just run off. It's not safe."

"Why not? You already took out the guy they sent after me. He's not a threat."

"I don't mean him. I mean other shifters."

"What?"

Tank curses, sticks his head in the other room to check on Mr. Unconscious, then returns and hauls me farther into the corner. "You're not pack. You have no protection. If you ran across a shifter's pack, they might come after you."

I blink. "What? Why? And how will they know?"

"Your scent. It's getting stronger. Every time you shift, until other shifters will know exactly who and what you are. And you won't have any protection. You have no people. You're alone."

Jesus. Like I needed the story of my life spelled out once again. I shrug him off. "Well, whatever. I'm used to that."

He presses his lips together, studying me. I meet his gaze, raise my chin. I've always been an outsider, a freak. He knows me a day and thinks I'm going to fall apart facing my problems on my own?

Fuck him. I've always been on my own.

"I'm going." I start for the door.

"You are not," he growls, grabbing my wrist.

"You don't get a say."

"You shifted for the first time in front of me. That makes me responsible for you." He seems to have just made that decision. His words shock me into stillness. "You don't want to go out there alone. Trust me."

"Well, I'm not staying here. My mom is in trouble. The goon in the other room is proof of that."

"Another reason you shouldn't be alone. He came here thinking he was going to confront a five-foot, hundred-pound woman he could easily overpower. And he would've if you'd been alone."

"Luckily, I wasn't. And I weigh a hundred and twenty pounds, thank you very much."

He shakes his head. "You're not going alone. It's not safe."

"Fine." I grin without mirth. "Then you come with me."

"I—" He stops. "Fuck." He looks down at his phone like it's an oracle with the answer.

"I'm going. You can either come with me or stay here with my unwanted guest." We both look at the still unconscious thug. Werewolves hit hard.

"Or I could tie you to the bed."

I don't dignify this with a response. It's all fun and sex games until you get a visit from a thug and a frantic call from your mom.

Tank reads this on my face and sighs. "Fine. But I'm in charge."

I blink. I never expected him to have my back. Relief rushes through me. "Okay, yeah. I'm getting used to that."

"Go pack." Tank jerks his head at my bedroom. "I'll take care of this guy."

"What are you going to do to him?"

"Wake him up and try to question him. I don't want you in here."

"Do you want me to get a tarp? In case there's blood?"

"No. I—"

A sound at the door makes both of us freeze. Someone's trying to get in. Keys jingle, and I hear a curse.

Shit. It's Benny. Good thing I changed the locks.

Tank starts for the door, a dangerous set to his shoulders. He's going to knock Benny unconscious.

"Wait." I catch his arm. "You can't—it's my ex-boyfriend."

"What?"

The doorbell rings. "Foxfire?" Benny whines. "I know

you're in there." He rings the doorbell a few more times and knocks. Jerk.

"He left stuff here. I've been on him to pick it up," I explain quickly.

"Fuck."

The mafia man is still sprawled on my rug. Fuck is right.

"I can stall him—" I start, when the thug begins to stir. At least until Tank's fist flashes out and catches him on the jaw.

"That's probably not good for him."

"He held a gun on you," Tank says. The flint in his eyes tells me in his world, you don't hold guns on women. You do pin them against a wall and spank them if they're naughty. It's a pretty interesting place, Tank's world.

"Foxfire!" Benny shrieks.

"Coming!" I shout, stepping in front of the window in case Benny decides to try to look through the curtains. "Give me a minute." I whirl to face Tank. "What are we—"

Tank already has the thug rolled in my rug and is carrying him to the back room.

"No, not there." I whisper. "That's where I keep Benny's stuff. Out back."

Tank heads into the kitchen.

The doorbell dings constantly.

"Go get the door," Tank orders. "Keep him occupied away from the windows."

I scramble back to the door, wrench it open, and slip out, pulling it shut behind me.

"What the hell?" My ex squints at me. It's not yet ten a.m. Early for him. In the daylight, he looks almost anemic.

"What do you want, Benny?" Weak chin, skinny, pothead. I have no idea what I even saw in him.

"I'm here to get my stuff. Whose truck is that?" He

scowls, pointing at the big gray truck with a covered bed in my driveway. "It's in my spot."

"You don't have a spot, Benny. I own this house, and we broke up."

"You got a man in there?" He frowns at the door.

"None of your business. I know you're here for your stuff, but I'm in the middle of something. Come back later." Out of the corner of my eye, I see Tank emerge from the side of the house, carrying the rug. He's headed down the driveway, to his truck.

"On second thought, now's a good time." I pull Benny inside before he has time to ask a question. "Here's your stuff."

"What happened to your rug?" he glances at the new bare spot in the middle of my living room floor.

"Termites," I blurt. "Rug termites." I grab the lava lamp from the corner. "Here." I hand it to him. "This is yours."

Benny frowns at it, which means he's not looking out the . window where Tank is loading a mafia man wrapped in a rug into the back of the big gray truck. Hopefully, none of my neighbors notices, either.

"I don't want this shit." Benny says. "I want my lights."

"What?"

"The grow lights."

"For my tomatoes?"

"No, you idiot, for my pot."

I suck in a breath. I knew he used but didn't know he grew. "Did you grow here?"

Benny rolls his eyes. "Where are they?"

I motion to the back room. "But what about my tomatoes?"

Benny rounds on me and starts in with that cutting,

derogatory tone he always used when he thought I was too air-headed, "Listen, dumbass—"

The next thing I know, Tank's in front of me. He has Benny by the collar and hauls him off his feet.

"Did you just call her dumbass?"

Benny splutters. "Dude—"

"You know this asshole?" Tank growls.

"Yeah, Tank! It's okay. He's my ex-boyfriend."

A louder growl this time, deeper in his gut. His wolf.

Hello, Wolfie.

"Apologize to Foxfire." Benny's eyes bug, but he says nothing, Tank bares his teeth. "Apologize."

"Jeez, I'm sorry, okay?"

Tank drops Benny, who splutters and backs up, wheezing. "What the fuck?"

"Does he have any right to this place?" Tank asks, his eyes on my ex.

"What? No. I own it. He was going to fix it up, though." It's probably the only reason I dated him." That, and he stuck around. In the early days, he made me laugh. After that, he was just a habit, one I should've kicked a long time ago.

"He accosted me!" Benny shouts, pointing.

"Yeah, I know," I scoff. "I was standing right here. Now, go away, Benny. Get your new girlfriend to buy you new grow lights."

"I'll call the cops on this place."

"What?" I gasp. "You grew the pot, not me."

"They don't know that. Like you said, you own the place."

"Get the lights," Tank murmurs, still not taking his eyes off Benny.

I trot to the back room, noting my returned rug, crumpled on the floor and missing the mafia man. I grab the pair of lights and return to find the two men in my life having a staring contest. If we assign points based on tough, commanding awesomeness, Tank is winning.

"Here." Tank takes them from me and shoves them at Benny.

"You call the cops, I find you," Tank says.

"Yeah, whatever, man."

Tank shuts the door in his face.

"You dated that thing?"

"Yeah."

"Break up with him?"

"Uh, yeah. He was bad in bed. And then I found out he cheated on me."

"He *cheated* on you?" Tank said as if I'd just claimed the sky was pink.

I nodded.

"If he bothers you again, you call me."

"Okay. What are we going to do about the wise guy?"

"He's in my truck."

"What about his car?"

"I'll take care of it. Get your things." Tank whips out his phone. "Hey, Nox? Yeah, I need a tow... Hang on." He pulls the phone away from his ear and smacks my ass.

Fresh tingles start there and race straight to my core.

"What did I just tell you to do?"

I roll my eyes. "Bossy! I'm going, I'm going." I spin on my heels and hustle to the bedroom to get my bag, feeling Tank's gaze on my twitching ass the whole way. Not sure why my foxy bits get so wet when he tells me what to do, but whatevs.

Twenty minutes later, Tank helps me into his truck and

shoves my bag behind the seat. The mafia man is in the covered bed behind us, duct taped within an inch of his life.

"Sure he'll be all right back there?"

Tank nods and turns on the truck. It roars to life, huge and powerful, like its owner. Tank's large hands turn the wheel. I get a thrill just watching him pull out of my driveway.

I bounce a little in my seat. "Road trip!"

Tank is silent. We head straight for the highway.

"Can we stop for snacks?"

"No."

"Okay." At least I have a water bottle. Although, I'd better save it for thirty minutes before we make a planned pit stop. I have a bladder the size of a pea.

I relate all this to Tank. His lips twitch, but he doesn't take his eyes off the road or change expression.

"How about music?" I hold up my iPod. "I have a great playlist. Do you have a way I can plug—"

"No."

"That's okay, I have speakers in here somewhere—"

"No. No music."

"Righty-ho, Big Daddy."

"Don't..." His thumb and finger touch his brows, and he briefly closes his eyes.

I grin at him, radiating *cute* vibes. They get me out of all sorts of trouble.

Tank sighs.

This is gonna be so fun.

~.~

Tank

A HALF-HOUR INTO THE JOURNEY, and I want to throttle her. Well, not really. I just want to shut that smart mouth up with my tongue. No, my cock. Actually, my dick wouldn't mind thoroughly claiming other parts of her. Every available orifice. That would be about the only thing that could put a dent in my bad mood. And blue balls.

But as hot as I find Foxfire, as much as my wolf is into her, I can't go all in with this girl. First of all, she's a little nutty. Adorably nutty, but still. She's the type my dad warned me about. He beat his variation of bros before hos into me so many times, I recognize the signs of getting swept away by a female.

Never put a female before the pack, son. They'll ruin everything for you.

I fear he's right. I'm already making bad decisions because of her. Garrett is in crisis right now, and I'm his second in command. I should be holding down the fort, checking in on Eclipse, and standing by for orders. Instead, I've wrapped a thug up in a rug and loaded him in my truck, and I'm driving four hours to Flagstaff.

Because of a girl.

Granted, she's a very hot, fascinating girl with the most fuckable mouth I've ever seen. But I can't go there with her.

Humming to herself, Foxfire props her legs on my dashboard. They are a mile long and all delicious bare flesh because she's still wearing those goddamn short shorts. I'm pretty sure if she keeps them up there, I will crash the truck trying to lean over and lick them.

"Legs off," I order. I sound grumpier than I mean to.

It doesn't affect her, except to turn it up a notch. "You got it, Big D." She slips them under her, grinning as if she lives to get a rise out of me.

"Don't get too comfortable," I warn her, but it's myself I'm giving a talking to. "We're going to get to Flagstaff, question this guy, and check on your mom." And be back before my pack wonders where I've gone.

I left a message with Garrett and tried Jared and Trey, but I've still heard nothing from them. It's a little worrying. But they're big wolves who can take care of themselves.

Meanwhile, I'm stuck on a road trip with Little Miss Sunshine. How did I get talked into this?

Oh yeah. Because my wolf won't let her alone. I can't stand a human male touching her, much less threatening her. And two humans already have in the past hour. A wolf shifter, even one from my pack? Forget about it.

"This is so exciting. My first road trip with a werewolf." She dances in her seat. She's taken off her hoodie, and her nipples press against the thin fabric of her shirt.

My cock wants to dance with her.

"Settle," I growl. What was I thinking, agreeing to being alone with her for a four-hour trip? She's a beautiful, foxy lady, and I'm a hot-blooded wolf. "We need to be careful. It's not a good idea to rile my wolf up."

"What? Why?"

"Full moon."

"What happens then?" Her voice drops. "During your time of the month?"

I snort at her term for it. "We don't have to shift, but we want to. Females usually go into heat."

"Like, get really horny?"

"Yeah."

"I get it. You're afraid you'll jump me. So what's the big deal?"

~.~

Foxfire

HIS HANDS CLENCH the steering wheel so hard, he's gonna leave imprints if he's not careful. "That's... not going to happen."

"Yeah. I'm hearing you don't want it to. What's the big deal?" I thought he could give it as good as he got it back at my place.

He mutters something under his breath.

"Wait, do you have a wife stashed somewhere? Little Tank babies?" My voice is light, defying the shrieking pain clutching my heart.

"No."

Relief. I try not to show it. I lean back with a smile.

"Look, this isn't a date. You're a shifter, and your mom's in trouble. We could be walking into a dangerous situation. We both need to keep our heads on straight." He looks at me like he's not sure mine is ever on straight. It's a look I'm used to receiving.

He must've seen a flash of hurt on my face because his gaze softens. "I think we can ask her about you being a shifter and get you to your kin."

Kin. I can't even wrap my head around that.

The highway signs flash by. We're approaching Phoenix.

"What about your pack?" I ask after a few minutes of silence.

"What about them?"

"I mean, they're like your family, right?"

"Closer than family. Pack is blood. Blood is pack," he recites.

"Right. Why not get them to help? You know, with—" I motion to the bed of the truck, where the gunman is tied and gagged.

"I don't need them to handle this."

"But what about Garrett? Don't you have to report to him or something?"

"Garrett's busy. One of our pack mates is missing, and he's searching for her. And no, I don't need his permission. He's the alpha, but he trusts me. I'm high enough in the pack, I only answer to him."

"There's a hierarchy."

"Yep. The more dominant your animal, the higher you tend to get in the pack."

"So where would I be in the pack?"

"At the bottom. You're small and a weaker shifter."

I slump a little.

"It's not a bad thing. All packs need submissive wolves. They hold the pack together. Dominant wolves, we fight all the time, learn our place. That's why roles in stable packs are strictly enforced. Otherwise, we'd tear each other apart. Submissive wolves don't pose that threat to dominant ones. We want to protect them."

"Do you want to protect me?"

His jaw clenches, and he doesn't answer.

He doesn't have to—I already know. He feels like he *has* to protect me. But he doesn't *want* to. My game of annoying him has been successful. I should be happy, right? This is a ploy I've used my whole life. Act weirder than they already think I am. Beat them to the punch of calling me freak. Own it.

Somehow it just makes me feel a little sick at the moment. What kind of woman does Tank prefer? I picture a tall, blonde she-wolf. I want to kill her. Maybe I'm not as submissive as he thinks.

I fall silent, mostly to give him a break.

As we push through Phoenix, Tank follows the signs to get on I-17 north to Flagstaff. He clears his throat. "In a few hours, we'll be in Flagstaff. Where does your mother live?"

"Um..."

He nods to the GPS. "Plug in the address."

"That's the thing." I wrinkle my nose. "She moves around a lot."

"Where's her house?"

"She doesn't have one. After I moved out, she downsized to an Airstream trailer. You know," I hasten to explain when Tank looks blank. "Those silver travel trailers people use to go camping cross country—"

"I know what an Airstream is. You're telling me your mother lives in one, year round?"

"Mmhmm."

"What does she do for work?"

"She's an artist, mostly."

Tank heaves a heavy sigh.

"I'll put in her last known parking place. She should be somewhere around Flagstaff. Sometimes she parks near the Grand Canyon to sell to tourists there."

"On a designated camping ground?"

"Uh, sure," I say in a tone that means *probably not.*

Another sigh.

"What are you going to do with this guy?" I hitch a

thumb behind me, indicating the truck bed and incapacitated thug.

"Going to question him."

"He's been out a while. Maybe you hit him too hard."

"He's fine."

Tank pulls out his phone.

A gruff male voice answers.

"Tank here. Do we still have the safehouse in New River?

"Thanks. I'm using it for the next two hours. I'll explain later." He hangs up, and for the next few miles, he looks so grim, I don't dare ask him anything. I hope he's not in trouble with his pack.

Thirty minutes out of Phoenix, something in the truck bed goes thump. And keeps thumping.

"Uh oh," I say as Tank swears. "I think the mafia man woke up."

"Too soon. Didn't dose him enough."

"Dose him?"

"Hang on." The hammering continues as Tank takes the exit.

"This was a damned stupid idea," he mutters.

I curl up on the seat. "Where are we taking him?"

"A safehouse. Private."

We're certainly in the middle of nowhere.

The banging has stopped. For now. "Did you really expect him to stay unconscious this whole time?"

"I dosed him."

"Dosed him?"

"Tranquilizer."

My eyebrows crawl up to my hairline. "You carry that stuff?"

"Yeah." He glances behind my seat where his black bag

lives, full of duct tape and heavy sedatives. "Werewolves aren't always in control. Sometimes their wolf... goes funny."

"Really?"

"Yeah. So we take precautions."

"Have you... dosed anyone before?"

"Yeah." He looks uncomfortable.

"Not just wolves," I guess. "Humans?"

"The world can't know about us."

I lick my lips. "Tank? Are you going to tell your pack about me?"

"Yeah. My alpha's out of town, but eventually I will report to him. I'll have to. He'll smell you on me and will want to know what happened."

"What will he do? Will he let me into the gang?"

"There's no gang. Just the pack."

"And?"

"Foxfire, I don't know. You're not a wolf, baby. To come into a pack, you need a sponsor. Someone to vouch for you. Otherwise, you're suspicious. A shy shifter like you—

"I'm not shy."

"Your fox is shy," he clarifies. "Shifters have rank in a pack. A new shifter has no rank. That means they're fair game for dominance attacks." He cuts a glance to me. "I'll explain more later."

"Okay. But if you tell the alpha about me... couldn't you be my sponsor?"

His fingers drum the wheel. "Maybe."

His reluctance hurts more than I care to admit. I've spent my entire life flying my freak flag, precisely because I know no one wants me in their club. I'm different. At least now I know *why* I'm different. *How* I'm different. But I guess it's too much to believe I'd fit in with other shifters just because I have a tail. They still don't want me.

We pull into a hidden driveway. Tank's shoulders relax a fraction. The thumping starts again. As we bounce down the gravel road, I hear muffled shouts. The thug must have loosened the tape over his mouth.

We ride around a wooded bend, and a tiny log cabin comes into view.

I gasp. "This is so cute."

"No one's supposed to know about this place except the pack."

"You gonna get in trouble for bringing me here?"

Instead of answering, Tank grabs his black bag and gets out of the car. I scramble to follow, but when we reach the trunk, he puts out his hand. "Stand back, baby."

I take a step to the side.

He starts to open the tailgate and pauses. "Go stand over there." He points to a rock a few feet away.

"Why?"

"You know why. It's not safe."

"He's already seen me."

Tank whirls and picks me up, carrying me until my back hits a tree. He presses his hard body against mine. "Baby, are you going to stay right here while I deal with him, or do I have to tie you to this tree?"

My foxy bits throb, nipples tighten. *Tie me up, big man.* My lips part, but no sound comes out. I'm staring at his lips, so supple considering what a manly-man he is. I want him to kiss me.

He does.

It's a hard, punishing kiss, and when he pulls away, his eyes gleam yellow. He points a finger at me, his lips quirking. "Stay."

I roll my eyes but obey, happy I have a front row seat. I

watch from a safe distance as Tank pulls open the bed, grabs the guy's feet, and yanks him out.

My gut clenches as Tank grapples with his captive, but he's a half a foot taller and fifty pounds heavier than the big thug. In no time, the man's on his knees, bound with tape.

"What the fuck?" the thug says.

"Shut up." Tank smacks him. "See this place?" he points. The truck is between the man and the cabin, so all he sees is wilderness around an empty road. "We're in the middle of nowhere. You have no rights. What did you want with the girl?"

"Foxfire Hines?"

Tank smacks him again. I cower a little; even though I know the controlled rage on Tank's face isn't directed at me.

"You don't speak her name. As far as I'm concerned, she doesn't exist for you after this moment."

"All right, all right! It was the job, man, the job." The thug babbles for a few seconds until Tank cuts him off.

"What job?"

"I don't know. I got orders—get the girl, tie her up, get her into the trunk, and take her to the drop-off."

"Who else?"

"No one else. Just the girl. And I wasn't supposed to hurt her, just get her to the place, alive. I don't know anything else, I swear."

The more the thug talks, the more Tank looks like he's gonna murder him. "Where's the drop-off point?" he growls in a voice barely human.

The thug names an address.

I scramble to write it down. As my pen scrapes, the thug cranes his head my way.

Tank smacks him again and puts a hood over the man's head, securing it with duct tape. The man struggles but ends up on the ground, hogtied and helpless. Tank leaves him on the ground and comes my way.

"Go wait in the cabin. The key is under the mat."

"You gonna torture him?" I whisper.

"No. I'll dose him and drop him on the edge of town. He doesn't know anything. I already sent his plates and information to someone who can get more info on him. He's a local thug, and he's telling the truth."

"How do you know?"

"I can smell it if he lies."

I shiver.

"Baby, go wait in the cabin."

When Tank comes in to get me, he's on the phone with someone named Jackson, reading off the address the thug gave us. "You can text me what you find."

I follow him out, and he motions for me to get in the truck. The thug is already in, the black bag behind my seat. "All right. Thanks."

"Who was that?" I ask when he hangs up.

"Friends. They're good at digging stuff up on the Internet. They're gonna look deeper and tell me what's going on."

"Werewolves?"

"Yeah, but not pack."

"You're helping a lot," I say as Tank climbs in.

He grunts and rummages around the scary black bag. I hold my breath, but he only tosses me a protein bar.

"Thanks. Got any water?"

Tank offers a bottle up but pulls it away when I reach for it.

"We're not stopping until Flagstaff," he warns.

I grin. "I just peed, but thanks for the warning." He rolls his eyes while I smirk, but I only take a few sips from the bottle before closing it up. No sense stopping while we have a drugged guy in the back.

We're off the main route now, taking back roads. Trees whip by. How many wolves roam this national forest? Coyotes? Foxes?

"You said before that my fox is shy?" I ask.

"I think she hid until she knew it was safe to come out."

"How did she know it was safe?"

He doesn't answer.

"Was it because she sensed your wolf? Or was scared of your wolf?"

More miles go by. Tank's profile doesn't change. Apparently, threatening a thug and going to save my mother isn't the bonding experience I thought it was. If anything, he looks more closed off.

"Look," I sigh, "I know you hate me, but—"

"I don't hate you."

"You think I'm annoying, then."

His head jerks *no*.

"Then what is it? Why won't you talk to me?"

"It's better this way," he mutters.

I put my hand on his leg, and he catches my wrist. Shards of glass pierce my gut. I try to hide it, but Tank glances over, and his grip softens as he reads my disappointment.

"Baby, it's not you," he says. "It's just better if we don't get involved."

"Tank, we're driving to my mom's in Flagstaff with a thug in the back. You spent the night last night. You saw me shift for the first time, stood up to my ex, and showed me a werewolf safehouse." I sit back in a huff. "It's too late to not be involved." I free my hand and do air quotes around *involved*.

He shakes his head, but his lips turn up a little. My little rant made him smile.

"What's so wrong about us being involved anyway?"

Wrong question. Every bit of warmth leaves the cabin. Tank might as well have turned to stone.

"Tank?"

"It's not safe," he says.

"What's not safe? You and me?" I snort. "That's ridiculous. You're the safest guy I know."

"No I'm not."

"Are you telling me I'm in danger? I can't see you hurting a woman."

"Not any woman. I'm only dangerous to you."

"What?"

He mumbles something, and I lean forward. "I didn't catch that."

"My wolf is attracted to you."

Ahhh. If I were a cat, I'd purr. "Your wolf? Or you?"

I put my hand on his leg, again.

"Stop it," he says. But he doesn't push it away.

"I never thanked you for helping me. I'd be a mess without you."

"You are a mess."

I laugh, but it's a harsh, bitter sound. "The word you're looking for is *freak*."

"You're not a freak." He frowns.

~.~

Tank

. . .

FOXFIRE cocks her head to the side as she studies me. I wonder what she sees. "You think I'm cute, though."

I shake my head.

"Oh, come on. You like me. Admit it."

"No."

Disappointment rumples her face. Immediately, I want to take it back. But what am I going to say? *Annoy me all you want, baby. Just be ready to face the consequences.* Fuck. The thought of pinning her down and teaching her to yield has my cock painfully pressing against my jeans.

Miles pass. Foxfire looks out the window, despondent.

"You're way beyond cute," I admit. "You're blazing hot."

"Really?" She brightens.

"Yeah. I'm trying very hard to keep my wolf from throwing you down and fucking you senseless."

"Awesome," she breathes. Totally mental. "I knew you wanted me." She gazes at me, head cocked to the side.

"What?" Her look makes me nervous.

"How about right now?" she asks. She puts her hand on my thigh and slides it up slowly. The truck swerves, and I grip the steering wheel harder.

"What? No."

But she's undone her seat belt and is sliding off her seat.

"Foxfire. No. Get back. I mean it."

"I never thanked you for helping me," she purrs. Leaning forward, she undoes the button on my jeans.

My cock leaps. Fuck, am I going to let her do this? We're on a back road in the middle of the national forest, no cars in sight, but still. The chances of me smashing the car into a tree the second she touches me are through the roof.

Small hands tug at my jeans. I shift to accommodate her fingers before I know what's happening.

I slow, but there's no shoulder on this stretch of road. Meanwhile, she grips my cock.

Fuck. This is happening.

"I can't," I rasp. Can't stay in control. Can't drive the truck and have her sweet little mouth on my dick. Can't keep from fucking her senseless. I catch her wrist in a firm grip, not too tight. I don't want to hurt her.

"Please, big man," she whispers, and I almost swerve off the road.

She gazes up at me from her knees, her slender fingers stroking my dick.

"Please." She licks her lips. "I want it so bad. Let me give this to you."

As if any male alive could ever deny her when she begs like that. Her sweet little nipples are hard as she pleads for my cock. She leans close and blows her hot breath over my manhood. My balls tighten to the point of pain. I'm so fucking hard. I've been hard ever since I first saw her.

The road widens ahead. Thank fuck. I roll to a stop and lift my hips. "All right. Take it out."

She jacks my cock slowly. Her small hand barely fits around it.

I put the truck in park and grip her hair. If we do this, we do this my way. "I want your mouth on me."

"Okay, Daddy." It's so twisted that she calls me that, but my wolf fucking loves it. He wants to take care of her, protect her, show her what it means to be her daddy—in the dominant boyfriend sense, not the fatherly sense.

She dives forward, swallowing my cock in her hot mouth. Just the right amount of pressure, tongue lolling. It's perfect, but I want to see how far she'll let me go, how she responds to the dominant side of me.

I tug her hair and pull her off. "Lick up and down."

"Yes, Daddy-o," she breathes. Okay, that's definitely wrong. But fuck if it doesn't get me harder. She licks me with lots of tongue, following my direction. She has an eager little mouth. I wanna make this last as long as possible. But she's not making it easy.

"Suck me," I order.

"Mmmm." She suctions her lips around my width and pulls more vigorously, sliding down my pole.

Totally submissive. My wolf is going wild. He wants to mark her right now, right here.

She's the one, he howls.

"That's right baby, take it far as you can go."

She swallows me deep, then pulls off, gasping.

"Good girl." I stroke her hair. I let her take her time before she tries again.

I slip a hand into her shirt, pushing down her bra to cup her tit. She's soft and warm, her tits a perfect handful. I brush my thumb over her nipple, and she shifts restlessly.

I squeeze her breast. "Suck me."

Her head bobs up and down in rhythm.

"That's it, baby. I'm close."

She applies herself with more vigor.

"Touch my balls. Cup them." She does, lightly fondling them. They tingle and tighten.

"Fuck, I'm gonna come. You ready, baby?"

I expect her to pop off, but she keeps sucking frantically. "Mmhmm," she agrees.

Fuck. Fuck. My sac tightens. Lights explode behind my eyes.

Foxfire. *Fuck.*

I pump into her mouth. She swallows it down, greedy little noises escaping.

"Fuck, baby," I gasp. "That was good."

She smiles up at me, a little angel with messy rainbow hair. Her lips glisten.

She's so goddamn fucking beautiful. I want to lay her out on my car hood, open her legs, and return the favor.

"Any time," she says just as a siren flares behind us. Blue and red lights flood the car.

The cops. *Fuck.*

~.~

FOXFIRE

UH OH.

I slip into my seat, wiping my mouth. That was so hot, I could've come just from sucking him. Insane.

Tank zips his pants, still cursing. The cop is getting out of the car.

"Seatbelt," Tank orders as he gets his registration and driver's license ready. I buckle myself in, wondering how obvious I look with my wet lips and disheveled hair. Whatever. Worth it.

I put on my innocent face as the cop approaches. Hopefully, the thug doesn't wake up and the cop won't decide he wants to search the covered truck bed.

We just have to act natural.

"Hi, Officer." I wave as the trooper leans in at the window.

Tank's jaw clenches, but he says nothing.

"You run into some trouble, son?"

"No." Tank doesn't look at the trooper. His hand flexes on the steering wheel. The cop's eyes narrow as he takes in the tattoos, the giant muscles and lack of respect for authority.

"No trouble at all," I trill, smoothing my hair. "It's totally my fault we had to pull over." The trooper fixes his eyes on me. "Um... I dropped a contact. It's silly, but I went down to look for it. He pulled over to help me." I flutter my lashes. The cop looks from me to Tank and back again. "So, it's my fault. He wasn't too happy at first," I whisper like I'm letting the cop in on a secret. "I kinda lose them a lot." I shrug, cock my head to the side, and giggle. Cute, clueless, manic pixie dream girl—that's me!

"You need to keep your seatbelt on, miss."

"Oh, I know." I nod, my eyes big. "He wouldn't let me go down until he pulled over."

Tank sighs on cue. I see the moment the cop starts to feel sorry for him, but also a little envious.

"Anyway, he's cranky," I babble on. "I promised I'd cook him a big dinner, but it looks like we'll have to do drive-thru instead. I'll have to make it up to him later." Another shrug and clueless giggle.

Now the trooper is fighting a grin. He glances at Tank's credentials and hands them right back. "This shoulder is for broken down cars only. You'd better move on now."

"Okay, thank you, Officer." I nod, my hair bouncing around my shoulders.

The trooper pats the side of the truck with his hand. "You drive safe."

"Yes," Tank mumbles, not quite deferential.

"Thanks, so much." I wave hard enough to jiggle my boobs.

As soon as the trooper is back in his car, I sag back in my seat. Crisis averted. No thanks to the sullen werewolf next to me.

"He was cute," I say as Tank pulls onto the road. He casts a glare on me that could turn a lesser being to stone.

I just smile. "But not really my type." I replace my hand on his thigh, stroking the hard muscle through his jeans.

He shakes his head. "Baby, you are big trouble."

"Mmm hmm. You gonna punish me?"

He looks over, disbelieving, like it's way too soon for me to make jokes. His eyes slide down. My bra cups are still under my boobs, pushing them up into some nice cleavage. The straps have slid half down my arms.

No wonder the cop let us off easy.

"I'm *definitely* punishing you, baby." His tone makes me shiver.

I go to adjust my bra, and Tank growls. "Leave it."

All righty, then. Something tells me whatever *punishment* is, it's gonna be hot. Even if Tank can be a little scary. I'm not worried.

Besides, his expression of bliss when he came in my mouth...worth it.

6

T *ank*

I STOP BRIEFLY, to drop the sleeping thug off in the woods behind a gas station. I leave some extra cash in the guy's wallet and prop him against a tree.

Foxfire's quiet as I turn the truck in the direction of the last-known whereabouts of her mother's trailer.

I can't figure out how she makes me do such crazy things. Like letting her blow me while I'm driving. With a mob enforcer in the bed of the truck. And a suspicious cop ready to look in the window.

Fates, it's a goddamn miracle I'm not in a jail cell right now for kidnapping and assault. My dad always warned me, "Females are our downfall. Mark my words, son, so you don't find out the hard way." He didn't mention how he learned the hard way. He didn't have to.

"There it is." Foxfire sits up straight, pointing to the

silver bullet-shaped trailer on the edge of national forest land. "But her vehicle isn't there, so I don't think she's home."

"Seriously?" I mutter. The trailer has a field of poppies painted on its side. Granted, the poppies are beautiful—very intricate and artistic—but still. Foxfire's mom is a total hippie. Now I know where Foxfire got the crazies.

"What's wrong?"

"Nothing. How long has she been here?"

"A few years. She likes the energy." Foxfire goes to open her door, but I motion for her to stop.

"Wait here, baby."

For once, she doesn't give me any lip.

I approach cautiously, sniffing the air. Incense, lavender or some other hippie oils. Normal human smells, blended with the wilderness scent. But something else. Cigarette ash.

"Is your mom a smoker?" I ask when I go back to the truck.

"You mean, like, pot?"

"Tobacco."

"No way."

"When did you last see her?"

Foxfire thinks for a bit. "Maybe last Thanksgiving? Or the year before that. Wait, what year is it?"

"Never mind."

I open her door.

"Thank you." Her cheeks color. Her nipples press against her shirt. I've got to get her thicker clothes. No one should see that sweet body but me.

Not that I'm claiming her.

She grabs a jacket out of her bag and tugs it on. She's still in her Daisy Dukes, so she looks fully ridiculous. And hot.

As we approach the trailer, the door creaks open.

"Mom?" Foxfire calls.

I hold out my hand to stop her. "Does she usually leave it wide open?"

"Not usually, but she rarely locks it. Says anyone who steals from her needs it more than she does." Foxfire shrugs. "She doesn't own much."

Lots and lots of wind chimes, and dream catchers hung from the awning and in the trees around.

I walk inside. The place is a wreck. Not just messy, but trashed. I'm about to ask Foxfire if this is typical of her mom's housekeeping when she lets out a sob.

"Mom?"

We search, but no one is there. I try to get a scent of the place, but it's too clogged with the smell of burnt sage. I cough and step outside to clear my head. That's when I notice what's in the dirt beside the door.

Bootprints.

"Does your mom have a man?" I ask Foxfire when she wanders out. "Someone who smokes?"

"She'd never date a smoker. She hates Big Tobacco."

I show her the prints with the cigarette ash. "Someone was here."

"They came for her, like they came for me. She's in trouble, Tank. I know she is."

"Maybe not. You said her car isn't here, right? Maybe she's hiding somewhere." I wrap my arms around her. I want to comfort her, but all I can think about is how Foxfire is with me, safe, when she would otherwise be in danger.

It takes me a moment to realize she's pushing at my chest.

"Let me go," she says and takes all the space I give her. She wraps her arms around herself and walks away.

Damn, she blames me. I kept her from getting the phone call from her mom last night.

"Foxfire—" I jog to catch her arm, but she twists it out of my grasp.

I release her, let her scuttle away. I don't want to hurt her. I want to comfort her.

"Leave me alone," she snaps and runs toward the pine trees.

"Foxfire, *no.*" I use every ounce of alpha command I can muster. She can't turn into a fox. Not here—there are cars zooming by just a few hundred feet away.

I find her facing a tree, her fists clenched.

"Come on," she whispers. "Come on."

She's calling on her fox, but her animal won't give her release. Not until I allow it.

"Foxfire, it's okay. We'll find her."

"She's my *mom.* She's the only family I have. If something happened to her, I have no one. No one. I'm all alone."

"Hush." I pull her into my arms, scoop her up to carry her back to the truck. Without thinking, I kiss her temple. "You have me."

~.~

Foxfire

I watch mom's trailer disappear behind us as we drive away. It's chilly, but that's not why I'm shivering.

I couldn't shift. My fox sits inside me, waiting, but she

wouldn't come out and let me escape my panic for a moment.

Figures. I'm a freak of a human, so why wouldn't my fox be broken? Foxfire, a shifter who can't even shift.

I barely notice where Tank is driving until he parks on a forest road. We're not in Flagstaff or near civilization.

"Come on," he says.

"Where are we going?"

"We're going for a run."

"Here? Now?"

"This is a national forest."

"It's almost dusk."

He pulls his shirt off and tosses it in the front seat. "We'll run in the moonlight." He strips out of his jeans. My mouth goes dry. "You coming?" He's almost naked.

"You should take your clothes off first. Less wear and tear. Trust me."

I give him a small smile.

It's chilly in the cool spring air.

"Come here." He gathers me in his arms.

He's so strong and warm. Super warm. After a minute, I relax against him.

"There you go, baby," he murmurs.

I shut my eyes and melt into his strong arms. A barrier between me and the world. A girl could get used to this. If I'm smart, I won't.

"You ready?"

"I can't. I can't do it."

"I know. I stopped you back there with alpha command. You were panicked, and it wasn't a good idea. But we're safe here."

Safe. With Tank.

"I don't... I don't know—"

"Call her, baby. Call your fox. Just relax."

"What if she doesn't come?"

"She will." He dips his head and kisses me. When his lips break away, his eyes glint amber. "*Now, Foxfire.*" His voice holds that same authority he used before.

My body shivers at the order, and he steps away.

The world changes. The cold and my chilled flesh swirl away. I'm on all fours, low to the ground, but it feels right.

I blink at the giant black wolf with yellow eyes facing me. He trots over and licks my muzzle until the tingles are out of my limbs. I take a step, hesitate. Tank nudges my side.

And we're off. Running. Sometimes Tank's in the lead, sometimes he's behind me.

I race, but I take many steps to his single loping stride.

I find a few tight places to hide, but he flushes me out.

The sun dies, and the moon rises. The chill bites through my fur, but it feels good. Makes me want to hunt and feast before burrowing and curling up in my den.

Wolf runs alongside, bumping lightly against my shoulder. He wants me to turn back. I feint and dodge him and keep running. He knocks me off my feet, stands over me. His growl rumbles through me.

I roll on my back, tilt up my neck, offering my vulnerable side in submission. He licks my face and raises his head. With a groan, he morphs into a man, still crouching over me.

"Come on," he says. "Back to the truck."

Still in fox form, I rise to my feet. For a second, I consider darting into the darkness. He couldn't chase me.

A large hand grabs the scruff of my neck, and I yelp. Tank lifts me and fixes me with a dominant stare. I hang limp as a kit.

"Back to the truck," he orders again and drops me on all fours.

I trot beside him obediently and hop into the truck bed when he opens it. After tugging on his jeans and laying a blanket over the cold metal, he climbs in after me.

"Shift, Foxfire," he commands, and my body obeys. For a brutal moment, the world contorts, every inch of me changing with a shock of sudden pain that leaves almost as soon as it came. I hadn't noticed the pain last time. When it's gone, I lie on the blanket, my limbs jerking with the sensation.

"It's okay, baby," he murmurs but doesn't touch me. I'm grateful. My skin is so sensitive.

He pulls out a meat stick, holding it for me to take a bite. He hands me a water bottle and finishes getting dressed while I sip.

Finally, I find my voice.

"Cold." I shudder.

He sets my clothes down beside me and pulls me into his arms.

"You did good, baby."

Twenty minutes later, I sit at a picnic table inside a barbecue place while Tank orders. He comes back carrying enough food for six people, including extra containers of meat.

I grab one immediately and dig in without bothering to add sauce. "So good." My fox is happy. Tank follows suit, eating steadily through a container of meat, then starting on a sandwich. He throws away the buns. If anyone's watching, they must think we're half-starved hikers on some crazy high protein diet.

Tank opens the last container, and my eyes light up at the rack of ribs. He waits until I've had my fill before he gestures for me to slide the container over. He picks through it, strips the rest of their meat, and gnaws the bones while I lick my fingers, content.

"Full," I tell him, and he gives a satisfied grunt. He watches me as he finishes off the ribs, and I get the feeling he wants to devour me.

Happy shiver.

I go wash my hands and refill my drink. When I return, he snags me to his side. He sits straddling the bench, pulling me in so my back is to his front. I protest a little when he steals a sip of my drink, but mostly I lean back, content.

Outside the window hangs a swollen moon and a sky full of stars.

Tank is large and solid under me. His hand splays across my midriff, rubbing absently. I really like cuddling with him.

"I never would've thought you were so touchy-feely."

"Mmm. It's a wolf thing."

I smile to myself. Yeah, right.

"We like touch," he continues. He speaks in a low voice because there are people around. I get a thrill of being included in the *we*.

"I've never been that into cuddling."

"You've never been around your kind."

"Will I ever be able to... make the change... on my own?"

"A little practice, You'll be fine. This is harder for you because you weren't raised around your kin."

"I'm glad I have you."

He doesn't say anything.

Ouch.

Right. He might be with me in this moment, but he makes no promises.

My stomach tightens, but I shrug it off. I'll just have to take what I can get. "I had fun tonight," I tell him.

He grunts. "You're just as naughty a fox as you are a human."

I grin at him.

He shakes his head, lips quirking.

"You gonna punish me?"

"Yep."

Squee!

7

F *oxfire*

WE FIND A HOTEL IN TOWN. "Wait here." Tank heads to the lobby. I stretch and drink the rest of my water.

My door opens, and Tank offers his hand. "Time to get out, baby," he murmurs. His voice is all sexy deep. I want to wrap it around me like a blanket. I love that he calls me *baby*, almost as much as I love seeing the conflict in his eyes when I call him *Daddy*. It's one part pure lust, one part shock, one part guilt.

"I have to make a call," Tank says as he opens the lobby door for me. "You gonna be good and stay put?"

"For now." I shoot him a sly grin. I go to flip my hair back and end up pulling a few stray pieces of grass out instead. "I want to clean up, anyway."

He nods and leaves me be. I decide to go full force, taking a mini shower and then carefully combing my hair.

The hotel has an old time-y theme, with pictures of pioneers and a few wagon wheels hung on the wall.

I eye the solitary bed. It's a sturdy thing made of real wood, only missing a quilt. I should offer to get a separate room, but I can't bring myself to suggest it.

Tank returns with his black bag and sets it on the floor while nudging the door shut with his foot. He rubs his face and then tugs off his shirt.

Suddenly, I'm wide awake.

"Damn. Are all werewolves so ripped?"

Tank glances at his impressive self before grabbing a water bottle and downing it. "Yeah. Our metabolism does it."

"You should turn Eclipse into a male strip club. You'd make bank."

Tank frowns.

"Just saying. I'd work there... for free."

"You're not going to be looking at any other wolf," he growls. "Not while you're with me."

I blink. I didn't realize I was with him, but I like the sound of it.

"For example, flirting with that cop this afternoon. Big no no."

I hide a smile, feign innocence. "But—"

"I mean it." His stern *naughty Foxfire* gaze makes me shiver.

Werewolves are possessive. Good to know.

"In fact, flirting with anyone in front of me earns you punishment."

I lick my lips. "This punishment. Am I gonna like it?"

His lips twitch. "Yeah, baby, you're going to love it. You're a submissive, through and through."

"How do you know?"

His voice grows deeper. "I can smell your arousal from here." He saunters slowly toward me.

I sit on the edge of the bed and twitch my legs together for relief.

When he reaches me, he grasps both my knees and shoves them wide. "*This pussy.*" He stares at the apex of my thighs as if he could see through my jean shorts. The jean shorts that I should've left in Tucson, because I've been freezing my ass off at the much higher elevation of Flagstaff.

I fall back onto my elbows. My breasts lift and fall with my panting breath. "What about it?" I whisper.

He crouches down and gets eye level with the seam of my shorts. Leans in and uses his teeth against my most sensitive bits. "*This pussy* is wet right now just because I'm bossing you around. Isn't it, baby?"

"Yes." I say it on an exhale, so it sounds like a gasp.

He stands, pushing my knees back so they roll up to my shoulders. I lie flat on my back, offering up the goods like a submissive pup. He looks down at me, eyes glowing amber. "Show it to me."

"Wh-what?"

"You heard me. I want to see that pussy begging for her punishment."

OMG. Did he just personify my pussy?

I'm beyond turned on. There's a rushing sound in my ears; my vision is going hazy. I fumble with the button of my jean shorts.

"Good girl," Tank purrs.

Flicking it open, I wiggle the fabric down my legs.

"Are you... are you not wearing underwear?" he asks in strangled voice. Apparently, he didn't notice when we stripped to shift. He takes over when my shorts are mid-thigh, pulling them the rest of the way.

"I don't like them."

"I should punish you just for that. Naughty girl. Keeping that bare pussy so close to me all day long."

"That makes no sense, wolf-boy."

"That's it, little fox." He scoops his forearm under both my knees and pulls them up and to the side. I'm confused until his hand claps down on my now exposed ass. I squeal. He lands a few more swats, one on each side and one in the middle.

Holy mother of god! In this position, he can spank not just my ass, but my pussy, too, which protrudes between my legs.

His lips quirk up, and I know he's noticed the moisture leaking from my foxy bits. He brushes his thumb lightly over them.

I jerk, every nerve ending lit up and sensitive.

"Are you beginning to see how this works, little fox?" He strums my bits again.

I'm forgetting my own name. "How what works?"

"Who's on top here? And who's on the bottom?" He smacks one cheek a couple more times, but he's far more interested in making me shiver and tremble as he pets between my legs.

"I'm not ready to concede anything." My voice sounds shaky, and considering my position, I don't think he's buying it. "I-I still have rights."

"What rights?" He smirks. "I'm bigger than you."

"That's not fair."

"That's how it works. I'll treat you right, baby. If I give you orders, it's for your protection, not because I have a hard on for control. Dominant wolves want to protect the weak."

"So you *do* want to protect me?"

"I *have* to protect you. It's a compulsion."

Disappointment spears through my haze of lust. It's

what I feared—he doesn't want to be here with me, he's just honor bound.

"So, when I give an order, you obey."

"Yes, Daddy." My tone is a touch snide.

He lifts my knees higher and delivers several more smacks, harder this time.

I yelp. "Tank—"

"It's okay, baby. Take your punishment, and I'll take care of you."

"Please," I gasp when he smacks particularly hard. It's not so much I can't take it, but I am super-duper turned on and don't quite know what to do with that.

"You gonna be a good girl?"

"Yes, please. I'll be so good."

"You gonna do what I say?"

"Yes, big man."

"Fuck," he mutters. His cock bulges in his jeans. I'm not the only one affected by this.

He stops spanking me but rests his hand on my bottom, squeezing absently.

"Fuck," he repeats. "I can't believe you aren't wearing underwear."

He rubs his thumb over my slippery flesh and finds the sweet spot. He uses the lightest feather-touch along my aching bud. I suck in a breath, and he stops.

"Did I hurt you?"

"Uh no. It's just—" I'm so sensitive. I was working and focused for so long, my foxy bits were ignored. "It's been a long time."

"Baby," he murmurs and lowers my ass back to the bed, releasing my knees.

When he brings his fingers back between my legs, I catch his hand, pressing my fingers over his. I show him how I like it, not that he doesn't seem capable of figuring everything—and then some—out on his own. "Please don't stop."

"I won't stop." His voice sounds even deeper than usual. "Play with your breasts," he orders.

I relinquish my pussy to his care and slide my hands up inside my T-shirt, under the cups of my bra. Imagining my fingers are his, I pinch my nipples, tugging them, giving a little pain with the pleasure.

I lose my inhibitions and rock against him.

"That's it," he murmurs. "Take it, baby. Take what you need."

"Fuck," I gasp. "I'm gonna come." I rock my hips harder, grinding against his fingers as my orgasm washes over me.

"Stay where you are," Tank commands, standing up. I sprawl before him, my legs spread. He tugs me to the edge of the bed. I wrap my legs around him as he pushes his jeans down just enough to take his cock out and jack it slowly.

"Tank…"

"Touch yourself."

My hand creeps between my legs, and I do as he commands.

"Tell me when you're close." He catches my ankle. "Spread your legs wider. Give me a show."

My head rolls back at that. Fuck, obeying him is so hot.

"Tank—"

"You close?"

I nod.

"Stop, and take off your shirt. I'm gonna mark you. Not permanently, just with my cum."

I don't know what permanently even means, but damn, that's hot. I strip my shirt and bra off and scoot closer to the edge of the bed.

"Touch yourself again."

I do, keeping my eyes on his massive rod. His hand wraps around it, but mine barely fit.

Arousal stabs through me, and I moan.

"Don't come. Not yet," he growls.

"Please—"

He jacks faster. "I mean it, baby. You come before I do, and I'll spank your sweet little pussy."

Suddenly, I'm close, too close. Right on the brink. "Tank—"

He gives a deep groan. I crest again as he paints me with his seed.

"Fuck," I pant.

"Fuck," he agrees.

I laugh, but he's serious as he reaches out and smears his spend over my breasts. "Good, baby. Stay."

I sag back on the bed as he heads to the bathroom. The tap runs, and he returns with a cloth and cleans me. I smell like him. I love it.

I start to rise, but he stops me. "Stay."

"I want water." Seems like I'm thirsty all the time now that I've found my fox side.

"I'll get it."

I sit up anyway, if only to admire the taut ass of the man who just gave me the best orgasm of my life. He returns, and I drink the water, then test my wobbly legs on the floor. I'm relaxed, like I've had a full body massage. Spanking and orgasms. Miraculous.

Tank cleans up by rubbing a wet towel over his face and body. I know this is just a romp, but I can't help imagine what it'd be like to wake up next to this guy every morning. Not to mention go to bed with him every night.

I might not leave the bed.

But he's made it pretty clear he's not interested in a relationship. And he just purposely didn't go all the way with me, which means he's holding back for a reason.

"Hey." I touch my foot to his leg. "Can wolves get foxes pregnant?" It's my old defense mechanism. Say the thing that will make them run. It works.

He goes still.

"Kidding," I say quickly, but it's too late. When he turns, his expression is blank. The walls are back up.

"Foxfire—"

"Tank, I know this is all for fun." He looks annoyed at being interrupted, but I barrel on. "No strings attached. I'm not expecting anything long-term."

He watches me carefully. Werewolves can smell lies. Well, I'm not lying. I spread my hands and make my case. "I'm rebounding, remember? I just broke up with... with... um..." What was his name again? I sit blinking at Tank for a moment, drawing a blank until, finally, I remember. "With Benny. We were together for two years, so... yeah, that's a long time. Whereas this—" I wave my hand between us. "This is just for fun."

I hold my breath, waiting for him to confirm or deny. This isn't more than a passing fling... is it? Even if our chemistry is explosive and I'm starting to lean on him.

~.~

Foxfire

. . .

I DREAM of running through the long grass, chasing something small and tasty. The brush parts to reveal a barbecue sandwich. An obvious trap. I sniff around and finally pounce. At the last minute, I look up at the big bad wolf looming over me—

I jerk awake. It's early, but I slept well and am wide awake.

Tank's curled around me, a rather large part of his anatomy digging into my bottom. I don't remember falling asleep—or curling into his arms. He must have pulled me close afterward. Unless he's already awake?

I rub my backside against him. Impossibly, his cock grows bigger and harder.

I roll and take him in hand. "I'm horny," I tell him.

His brown eyes flit over me, his features a little softer with sleep. Handsome, but a bit more approachable.

I grin with all my teeth. "May I suck you?"

A pause, and then he moves in a blur. He flips me onto my back. "Don't want your mouth," he growls and spreads my legs. His head lowers to my pussy.

He licks into me, long, hard strokes that drive me toward Orgasm Town. "Tank," I chant, my knees swaying in the air. "Oh, Tank, oooh." As pleasure ebbs through me, he licks every bit of me clean, then climbs up and presents his cock. *Now* he wants my mouth. I crane my head to suck as much as he'll let me.

He leans over to the bedside. A crinkle of a packet, and he moves away from me, rolling a condom onto his giant, perfect, rigid cock.

Thank you, baby Jesus.

He picks me up and props my legs over his shoulders. When he sets the head of his cock at my entrance, I'm almost folded in half.

"Ready?" His gaze rolls over me, face no longer blank but heated, active interest there.

"Yes. God, yes." I grip the bedspread.

He slams into me, no holding back, no warmup. I'm soaking wet. My head flies back as he drills into me, but it's perfect. He draws out and does it again, the force moving me down the bed. I reach up and grip the headboard.

"That's it, baby. Hold on."

He fucks me hard, punishing thrusts that drive me closer to orgasm. He drives fast.

"That's it. Hold on, baby."

He grips my legs. I was wrong—he was holding back. pummeling my lower half. His giant cock fills every bit of me. My orgasm blows up, ready to envelop me.

"Wait for permission," he reminds me.

"Please, oh please—"

"No." He squeezes my ass. "Hold off."

"Have to—" I protest, my orgasm so close I can reach out and take it.

"Now, baby." And I come, convulsing, body ablaze like I've been hit by lightning.

~.~

Tank

FUCK. Foxfire thrashes under me, her pussy spasming, gripping me. She's squeezes so tight, trying to snap off my dick.

"That's it, baby." I roll her nipple between my thumb and finger, pinching a little. She cries out again.

I pull out and flip her over, admiring the slight redness on her bottom. I cover her with my body, dragging her close with an arm around her middle. "You know what happens to naughty foxes?"

She's still crying out in the grips of orgasm. "They get fucked—hard."

I thrust into her from behind. She's so wet, I bottom out immediately. Holding her tight, listening for the slightest sound of distress, I plow her, taking care to swivel my hips and fill every part of her.

I cock one of her legs up and send my cock deeper. Fuck. I want to live inside her. I pause to slide my hand down her front, between her legs. Her pussy spasms as I find her clit.

"Oh no, Tank, please. It's too much."

"Take it, baby," I growl. "Come as much as you want." I pull my hand away and turn her over again. I want to see her, face flushed, hair mussed, big eyes filled with stars, looking at me like I'm a hero. She doesn't disappoint. She has that hazy just-fucked look, but her eyes snap eagerly to mine, and she bites her lip. She wants more.

I bend over her, pulling her into position. I close my teeth over her breast and scrape my teeth over her nipple a few times before rising up to give her what she needs.

I'm half off the bed, standing on my right leg, one knee digging into the bedspread. I grab her legs and lift her to meet me. She wraps her legs around my middle.

I give it to her again, hard. With every thrust, the headboard goes thump, thump, thump, hitting the wall.

"Hang on," I order, and she reaches for the slats again, doesn't quite make it.

"Tank," she moans. "I'm coming—"

"Come for me, baby," I order and root myself deep. My cock pulses filling the condom, I wish for a second I was filling her pussy, burying my seed deep inside her. She should bear my mark, carry my pups.

I draw a hand over my face.

Fuck. Less than forty-eight hours, and I'm a goner. Foxfire is a drug, and I'm addicted.

We wash up carefully.

Foxfire pads around the room, touching random items and talking softly to herself. I imagine the pack witnessing a moment like this. Two things happen at once. My heart squeezes with a surge of protectiveness and affection for the princess of La La Land. And I see her through their eyes—the crazy girl who makes Tank lose his good sense. Lose his place in the pack. Just like my mom did for my dad. Am I ready for that consequence?

Fuck, no.

But the thought of leaving her brings on the weight of a giant boulder crushing my chest.

"Tank?" she calls, and I'm halfway out of the bathroom before she finishes her sentence. "You need to see this."

She crouches next to the bed.

I pull the toothbrush out of my mouth. "What? What is it?"

Foxfire look up with a guilty expression. "Here." she gestures. I come around the bed to see what's wrong.

"What is it?"

Foxfire lays her hand on the frame. "Right here." A crack in the wood. The slat is sagging. "We broke the bed."

She puts her hand on it, and the thing groans, creaking lower under the strain. One corner of the bed does look lower than the rest. The bedclothes are strewn halfway across the room. The picture above the bed hangs askew. Her eyes dance with merriment.

This is what she's done to me. My neat, rule-abiding life looks like a hurricane just roared through it.

We pack up and head out of the hotel, leaving a wad of cash on the comforter for the breakage. Foxfire's mom had better make an appearance soon because I can't stick around Flagstaff all week. Even if I'm already dying for another fuck session with Foxfire. But I can't keep claiming her like she's mine.

Hell, if she only knew how much I wanted to mark her in that bed. Not mark her with my cum, but with my teeth. As in, make her my mate for life. Which means...

My wolf has fallen, fallen hard.

So, why do I have this underlying dread about getting involved with her?

Oh yeah. Because of my mom.

8

T*ank*

"OKAY, let's figure out where your mom is," I say as I pull into a diner. It's still before nine a.m.

"Her vehicle wasn't at her trailer."

"Where does she work?" I park and get out.

"She teaches art at a community center and makes jewelry and other crafts to sell to tourists. Dreamcatchers, wind chimes, stuff like that."

"She makes a living doing that?"

Foxfire shrugged. "Enough. She's never held down a job, as long as I've known her. But the way she lives, she doesn't need much." We sit down and open our menus.

"The thugs who tore up her place—they probably spooked her. Does she have friends she could've run to?"

"I have no idea. Could you maybe sniff her out? You know"—she drops her voice–"in furry form?"

"In public?"

She shrugs. "I could get you a collar and leash."

"No."

"You have any better ideas?"

"We'll explore on foot. It's good for you to learn how to use your nose to track, in whatever form."

"Sounds good." We order, and the food comes and she tears into her plate. We both got extra orders of meat.

Under the table, Foxfire's foot rests on mine. When she finishes her meal, I slide her leftover sausage my way and dig in.

Her foot slides up my inseam, resting on my crotch.

"Careful," I growl at her.

She just smiles, the sweet curve of her lips making my dick hard. Naughty fox.

I ask the waitress if the cook wouldn't mind making a few burgers to go, although it's not their lunch hour yet, and after she brings them, I put them in the truck. When I turn around, Foxfire is heading toward a craft and farmer's market. It's early enough, it's sparsely attended. The booths are still getting set up.

"She used to sell here. I'm going to ask them if she's been around," she says when I catch up, growling at her for leaving without me.

I ask first. "Excuse me. Do you know where Sandra Hines has her booth?"

The man frowns at me.

"Sunny," Foxfire adds. "She goes by Sunny. My boyfriend hasn't met her yet." She grabs my hand, and the man's look of suspicion disappears when Foxfire adds, "She's my mom."

"Oh yes, Sunny. Usually, she's set up over there. Haven't seen her since Friday, though."

"Thank you." Foxfire tries to hide her disappointment, but I can see the devastation in her eyes.

Fuck. We have to find her mom.

~.~

Foxfire

We do a round of the market. I meet as many of the stall owners as I can. They all agree my mom often shows up to sell there, but not every day. I give them my cell number and ask for a call if they see her.

We take a break to step into a cell phone store. Tank buys me one to replace the one he crushed.

"So what now?" I ask as we leave the store and head for the truck. I lower my voice and wait until a few tourists pass before murmuring, "You wanna do the four-legged thing?"

"I'm not sure it will help. Your mom has been all over this town. Her scent is here. Besides, you have a phone now. if one of her friends spots her, they'll call you." He puts the truck in gear. "Let's try her house again, see if we sniff out any clues."

Back at the trailer, he shifts. I keep a lookout as a huge black wolf sniffs around carefully. It's amazing how big he is. Just massive. Real wolves are pretty large, but he's taller than them by a head.

He hops up into the bed of the truck and waits to shift back until I close it up. When he climbs out, fully clothed and breathing hard like he's run a four-minute mile, I hold up the burger I've unwrapped from its paper.

"Who's a good doggie?"

He snatches the sandwich from my hand and inhales it in one gulp. "Don't ever call me a dog. Not unless you want a red ass."

I hand him the bag with the rest of the food from the diner. "Wolfie?"

He shakes his head.

I lean against the truck bed, admiring the flex of his strong jaw as he chews. "I love teasing you."

"Keep it up, baby. There will be consequences."

"I love consequences."

"You don't have to tell me that. I've felt how wet your pussy gets."

"My foxy bits," I correct. "That's what they're called."

Tank shakes his head.

"You know you love it, Big Daddy."

"Keep talking, baby. I'll still be on top tonight."

I turn away to hide my happy grin. Tank finishes his food and uses a water bottle to wash his hands.

I flop onto the truck bed. "Now what?"

"There was something in the trailer. It smelled... I think you should see it."

Reluctantly, I follow him inside. I should've visited my mother more. She drives me crazy, but that's what family is about. Even though I never lived in this particular trailer, it smells like my childhood. There are a few things I recognize —the stained glass design I helped Sunny make, a small gold statue of Buddha, the Japanese tea set we bought at a thrift store.

"Here," Tank beckons. Beside a little bench used as a

seat and storage, he taps a panel and opens a hidden compartment. Out pours a stack of envelopes.

I pick through them. They're all addressed to Sunny, but only a PO box is listed as the return address. "They're empty."

"Recognize the address?"

"No. Why did you think these were important?"

"Because," Tank says quietly. "They smell like fox."

~.~

FOXFIRE

BACK IN THE TRUCK, I finger the address. We took one envelope and put the rest back.

At this point, it's my only link to my heritage.

It's lunchtime, and even though he's already eaten, when we stop for tacos, he orders twenty.

"We might try the community center. Find out if she still works there and if anyone's seen her."

I nod. I'm still thinking of those empty envelopes.

"It's okay, baby," he says. "We'll find her."

"Do you think someone...?" My throat clogs. Even if I don't visit often, Sunny is family. She's all I got.

"I think they scared her. She left a message for you, and she's lying low. Foxfire, she's not a shifter."

"But what about—" I lift the envelopes.

"Those are the only thing in there that smell like fox."

"She could be dormant, though. Maybe her fox is like

mine—she never felt safe, or protected enough..." My voice trails off at the pity in Tank's eyes. I can handle being called a weirdo or freak, but don't fucking pity me.

"I don't think she's a shifter. I think you got the gene another way."

That only leaves my male parent. My missing male parent. Is it possible? The one who made me a fox is the father I never met?

I don't realize I've spoken out loud until Tank answers. "I think it's the strongest solution. Either way"—he taps the envelope—"this holds the answer."

I trace the address again. Large, clumsy handwriting, almost childish, indicating an address in Moab, Utah. The postmark is from three years ago. All this time, and my dad was only six hours away?

It doesn't matter, I tell myself. All that matters is finding Sunny.

"Tank? What are we going to do when this is all over?"

His face goes blank. "Let's just take this one day at a time."

I open my mouth to protest.

"Foxfire?" A familiar voice wafts across the street.

A long-haired woman in a peasant blouse and skirt walks through traffic, completely oblivious to the cars slowing to avoid hitting her. One honks, and I wince.

My mother doesn't notice. At least I think it's my mother. She's dyed her hair blonde, with pink streaks, making her look younger. "It is you!" She gasps and rushes to me. "I thought I was seeing with my third eye."

"Sunny." I run to her.

"Darling!" About a hundred thin bracelets chime on her wrists as she throws her arms around me and hugs me tight, enveloping me with the scent of sage and lavender oil, and her own earthy smell. She still doesn't believe in wearing deodorant. Or shaving her pits. My super fox senses make that clear. Tank holds his hand near his nose, a stony look on his face. I grimace in sympathy and wipe my face clear of expression before Sunny lets me out of the hug.

"And who is this?" Sunny turns to Tank with a broad smile.

"This is Tank."

"Oh. what a lovely name. Are you two—?" She looks from me to him. I was expecting this.

"Yes," I say at the same time Tank says, "No."

Ouch.

"We're not in a traditional relationship," I explain. "We're just lovers." Beside me, Tank goes very still. I want to look at him but don't dare risk it.

"Oh, how wonderful." Sunny claps her hand with a tinkling bracelet explosion. "Love should be free from the constructs of society."

I grab Tank's hand. "That's what we thought. I mean, why label it? We're just having sex."

"Oh, good." Sunny lays a hand on Tank's broad chest. "Yes, I see. Your chakras are out of balance, though."

I cough. "They should be balanced. We spent all morning working on alignment."

Sunny closes her eyes. "Your heart chakra is damaged. An early wound, maybe? Something caused you to shut your heart to love."

"He's fine." I bat her hand from his chest, and she steps back. I scoot closer to Tank, who looks stunned. Maybe I should've taken the time to warn him a bit more.

"Where have you been?" I ask Sunny. "We went to your trailer and were worried."

"Oh." She waves her hand. "That was just a bit of trouble. Some men came by and said I owed them money."

"Well, did you?"

"I may have borrowed a bit to fix the bus last year. A Mr. Biggs. He's a nice man, runs a few card games."

"Mom!" I pull her into an alleyway so our conversation is private. "You got involved with the mob!"

"Really, darling? Well, you know, modern currency is a figment of our imagination. Someone should really explain that to these lenders."

"Mrs. Hines—" Tank begins.

"Oh, Sunny, call me Sunny. I insist."

"Your daughter had a visit from a thug. We think it had to do with your trouble."

"Oh!" Her hand flutters to her chest. "Are you all right?"

"Fine, Sunny." I sigh. My mom is so clueless sometimes. I must take after my dad. "Tank took care of him."

"Really?" Sunny brightens. "Is he swimming with the fishes?"

"Mom!"

"No," Tank says. "We did not kill him. We questioned him and let him go. Have you had more thugs bother you?"

"No, not since the first visit. "

"But your trailer was trashed."

"Yes, I think some kids did that. I've been meaning to go back and clean it up." She waves her hand to the chorus of bangles.

"You don't think it was the same thugs?"

"No, of course, not. I mean, I paid the loan back. Mr. Biggs said it would be all right."

"Then, why didn't you go back to the trailer?"

"Negative energy. I haven't had a chance to sage it and

clear dark energies that came in, so I slept the last couple of nights in Daisy."

"So you borrowed money, got a reminder, paid it back, but then your trailer was trashed. Did you call the cops?" Tank asks.

"No need, darling. The men who came had very bad energy. Karma will take care of them."

"Men? There was more than one of them?"

"Yes, two," Sunny says. "And they seemed interested in you, Foxfire. That's why I called to warn you." She looks back and forth between us. "Is something wrong?"

"Let's go back to your home, Ms. Hines. We have a few things to discuss."

9

F oxfire

"SORRY," I say as we drive over, following the brightly painted VW bus my mom calls Daisy. "I should've warned you about her."

"Has she always been this way?"

"When I was sixteen, she met the guy who wanted to take me to prom, gave him a box of condoms and a candle shaped like the Minoan fertility goddess."

Tank winces. I shrug. "I was used to her by then. She's a big believer in free love."

"So, your father..."

"They were twin flames." I mimic Sunny's airy tones. "Souls destined to meet. They met at some sort of festival, I think."

"So he could be the shifter."

"Yeah," I say quietly. My mom's anonymous sperm

donor, aka Dear Old Dad, gave me more than gray eyes and the tendency to burn in the sun.

Inside the trailer, Tank and I clean up while Sunny bustles about making green tea. Her bangles ring constantly until I ask her to remove them.

"Tank prefers silence," I explain.

"Does he meditate?"

"Yes," I lie.

Poor Tank hasn't said a word.

"Most days, he takes a vow of silence."

He snorts.

"Really," Sunny breathes.

I nod. "He broke it to be with me. After I got your voicemail—"

"Yes, I'm so sorry, darling. It just shook me."

"Of course." I hug her. The teapot whistles halfway through, but we remain in our embrace until Tank clears his throat.

"Right, silence," Sunny mutters. She serves the tea in traditional Japanese service, which means we get about a thimbleful each. Tank looks at his dubiously and doesn't touch it.

"So, Sunny, about these men—"

"They were very coarse, darling. I had a bad feeling and left in the bus immediately after talking to them. I came back to get my things and the place—" She gestures. My poor mom, all alone.

"Do you have any idea who they might be?"

"No, darling. I asked Mr. Biggs about them, and he said the matter was all settled, there must have been some mistake. It was all very strange."

"Huh," Tank says. "But you say they asked after Foxfire?"

"Yes. Perhaps they thought she had the money, if I didn't."

"Excuse me. I have to make a call." With a nod at me, he rises and leaves.

"Mom, I have to ask you something. It's about Dad."

"Your father?"

"Yes. How did you meet him?"

"The street festival. He manned a booth near mine. We spoke quite often and, well." She shrugs.

"Did he tell you anything? About himself or his family?"

"Only that they were very private. He grew up on a compound up in Utah. Sounded quite secretive. They weren't at all welcoming to outsiders."

"Did he..." I pause. I don't quite know how to say "turn into a fox every full moon?"

Tank returns to sit with me.

"Ms. Hines, your daughter is very special."

Sunny bobs her head. "Oh, yes. I know."

"We're wondering what traits she might share with her father."

"Do you mean his wild energy?"

Both Tank and I sit up straighter.

"Yes," I say slowly.

"You definitely share the same soul color. Sort of red... with gold. Vibrant. Pulsing energy."

"Yes, all right."

We give each other a glance. She doesn't know anything.

"Funny. But we had the wildest time together."

I clear my throat.

"Once we partied and he disappeared, and in his place —well, in his place was his spirit animal. At first I thought it was a bad trip. But your father was in tune, very in tune. What makes you ask about all this?"

I try to think of a logical way to ask without telling her I shift to a fox. "I want to know more about him. Recently, I—"

Tank shakes his head.

"Um, I'm going through a spiritual awakening. Finding my spirit animal, too."

"Ah." Sunny nods.

"Ms. Hines," Tank cuts in. "After you called, Foxfire was afraid for you. I thought it might be good if she learned more about her father."

"I just want to know if I have any family on that side, and I don't know anything about him, really."

"Of course. You just never cared to hear about him."

I blink. "I thought you didn't want to discuss him."

"Oh, I don't mind. Your father was very special. I'm glad our energies aligned to make a child. No, whenever I brought him up, you changed the subject."

"He abandoned us," I croaked. My throat is suddenly dry. I swallow my tea and reach for Tank's. He scoots it closer to me, and I down it, too.

"He didn't. His sensitive nature didn't allow him to live around people for long. All his kin were very secretive. He was the only one brave enough to venture out to market. The rest of them lived off the land. Before he hitched a ride to the market, he had never ridden in a car. But he was more modern than all his relatives combined."

"Did he ever ask about me?"

"I sent him notes and a few pictures. He only sent back money."

I pull out the envelope and set it on the table.

Sunny nods. "Darling, if I'd known you wanted to meet him—"

I turn away from her. "I looked up the address. It belongs to a Johnny Red."

Sunny nods. "Yes, that's him."

"That's him? My dad? He was in Moab all this time?"

"No, darling. He moves around quite a bit. At least he used to."

"But he has a post office box there?" Moab. A wilderness. Good for fox shifters.

Sunny hesitates. "Darling, are you sure—"

"Just tell me. Is my biological father currently residing a mere six hours away from here?"

My mom bites her lip and nods.

Suddenly the trailer, with my mother's scent and items from my childhood, is too close and stuffy to bear. "I need a moment," I whisper and leave. Tank stirs but lets me flee.

Outside, the chilly air has a bite to it, but I don't mind. I walk quickly to the edge of the woods and stop, chewing my lip. Sunny doesn't know I'm a shifter. Maybe no one does. All my life, I've marched to the beat of a different drummer. But now I really am alone.

My skin itches, like I could shift and run. Life is simpler as a fox.

"Foxfire," Tank calls. I don't turn around, even when his heat hits my back.

The wind picks up. I wrap my arms around my body but refuse to move.

Tank sighs. He stands beside me, keeping his eyes on the forest. His profile blurs out of the corner of my eye.

"My mom left, too," he says. "When I was nine. My dad was a wolf, had a good place in the pack, but she… she was a loner."

The wind blows along the trailer with a slight howl. I don't know whether it's creepy or comforting.

"Did you ever see her again? After she left?" My voice is brittle.

"No." Tank moves and puts his hands on my shoulders. "Whoever your dad is, he cared for you. He's been sending money all these years."

My cheeks are a bit wet. I dash at my cheeks. "He didn't care. He didn't stay. He didn't teach me who I am. I never thought..." I stop talking because, of course, I never thought anything like this would happen to me. I lived twenty-six years as a human. I embraced my weird. I just never thought I actually was a freak.

"Come here." Tank folds me in his arms. He's so big, for a second I'm completely enveloped, hidden from the world.

"It hurts," I whisper against his broad chest.

"Baby."

"He should've been here. He should've helped me." I wipe my eyes, annoyed. I never cared about my dad. He left. Why should I feel anything for a man who obviously felt nothing for me?

"I can't believe he didn't try to reach out, tell me he was a fox."

"Maybe he wasn't sure you were one."

"What do you mean?"

"Children of shifters and humans aren't always able to shift themselves. Maybe he thought it best to leave you alone, let you live a normal life."

"Normal life? Raised by Sunny?" I scoff.

"As a human, then."

"Well, so much for that," I mumble, but I'm not sorry I'm a fox. I refuse to regret my animal's magical presence in my life. It's not her fault my life is fucked up and my parents are a joke.

Tank regards me, but there's no pity in his expression. Only a tenderness that will make me strong again, if I let it.

He cups my cheek. "What do you want to do?"

I take a deep breath. "I want to find him."

"Okay," he says, and just like that, I feel better. But I don't let go of him. Tank's my rock, I decide. I'll cling to him, as long as he lets me.

~.~

Foxfire

"You sure about this, baby?" We spent the last few minutes informing Sunny of our plans and getting ready to head out. Tank has his arms around me again. I've needed more fortifying hugs in the past day than I have my entire life.

"Yeah. My fox... she needs her kin."

He nods.

The door to the trailer bangs open, breaking us apart.

"This is going to be so fun," Sunny trills from the front step. She's dragging a large carpet bag behind her.

"What is?"

"Road trip!" She claps her hands.

I roll my eyes. Mom can be so ridiculous. I definitely take after my dad.

"Where do you want this?" Sunny lifts her bag.

"No," Tank says.

"What?"

"Um, Mom," I rush in, "we didn't realize you'd be coming."

"Well, of course I am, silly. How else are you going to recognize your father?"

I look at Tank, who rubs his forehead. "I don't have room in my truck."

"Oh, I can ride in the back." Sunny waves a hand.

Tank shakes his head.

"Or we could take Sunny's bus," I offer. The three of us turn to look at Daisy. It's an old VW bus. The parts that aren't rusted are painted purple, with white daisies.

"What a marvelous idea!" Sunny crows.

Tank's jaw clenches as he closes his eyes.

10

By noon, we're on the road. Tank insisted on driving, even though he's twice as big as the seat. His big hands are monster-sized on the steering wheel. Before we left, Sunny insisted on burning sage and cedarwood throughout the vehicle to clear negative energy for our journey. The cabin smells of burnt herbs and spilled paint from her art projects. Even though Tank hasn't said a word, I can tell he's pretty close to the breaking point.

I decide to sit in the back with my mom to act as buffer.

"He has such masculine energy," Sunny tells me in a loud whisper. "Do you think he'll let me paint him?"

Mom paints nudes. "No, I don't think so. He's a very private person."

Sunny considers this.

"I wouldn't ask him," I add. "He gets... grumpy."

"You certainly have a way with him."

Me? "I don't know about that. He's kinda bossy." Especially in bed. Not that I'm complaining.

"I like him," Sunny decides.

I let Sunny read my palm. She's always been a tarot reader, and palmistry is something new for her.

"Interesting, interesting. You'll live a long life, darling, and have one great true love. You'll have some challenges along the way, but it'll work out in the end." She drops my hand, looking expectantly at Tank.

"What about a tarot reading?" I ask before she can grab his hand. Knowing her, she wouldn't care that he's driving a stick shift.

My request buys another few minutes of silence as Sunny digs in her giant sack-like purse for the deck of cards she always carries. This time it's not traditional tarot, but some kind of angel cards.

"You will go on a great journey—not in distance, but in importance."

"Makes sense," I agree.

"You will face a great enemy." Sunny frowns.

"I've always wanted a nemesis," I say absently.

"Darling, this is very serious."

"Oh, I know. I fear for my life every time I go to the bathroom. Toilet snakes."

"What are toilet snakes?" Sunny asks.

"They're snakes that come out of the toilet while you're sitting on it and bite you."

Sunny gasps.

"Foxfire," Tank rumbles.

"What?" I ask innocently.

"There's no such thing."

"Oh, I know that," I say. "I'm still scared of them."

His lips twitch.

"Speaking of toilet snakes..." Sunny says.

Tank sighs and takes the next rest stop exit. As Mom and I leave to go the bathroom, he pulls out his phone. I hasten through my business and leave Sunny admiring some murals.

Tank's on the phone. I approach slowly, giving him space until he thanks whoever he's talking with and hangs up.

Instantly, his eyes land on me.

I give a little wave and bounce to his side.

"I just called in a few favors," he tells me. "I have people looking into your father's whereabouts. By the time we reach Moab, we should know more."

"Thanks."

"Don't mention it."

"What about Garrett?"

"Haven't heard from him."

"Still? Is he usually this hard to get hold of?"

"No." He rubs the back of his neck. "I got a feeling—something's going on."

"Do you need to go?"

"I'm going to see this through."

A thrill goes through me. It shouldn't. He's not choosing me over the pack, not forever. But it stills feels good.

"Thanks."

He cups my chin for a moment and studies my face. He's going through all this trouble. I hope it's worth it.

I hope I'm worth it.

But even if I am, in the end, he hasn't made me any promises.

"So... my mother."

He just shakes his head.

"I'm really, really sorry," I begin. "She means well."

He grasps my nape and pulls my face up to his, claiming my mouth. His kiss is dominant, demanding. I can't decipher the meaning. Is this more punishment? Promise?

"Don't apologize again, baby. You can't help who your mom is. None of us can."

My mouth twists into a wry smile. "Well, my mom believes all babies choose their parents from the other side. We pick them for certain lessons we want to learn or something."

He frowns, shutters going down over his face again. He must be thinking of his own mom. What lessons—or scars —did she leave on him?

"Do you think she knows something? I mean, deep down? She did name me Foxfire."

"I don't know, baby." He rests his hand on the back of my neck and kneads it a little. I didn't realize how tense I'd gotten. "I wouldn't know what's going on in her head."

"I will say this. She's friendly. She's never met anyone she didn't like." Sunny is at a picnic table with a group of tourists. She's got her astrology book out and is doing their horoscopes. "Are you close with your dad?"

"Yeah. We were on our own for a few years, before we found Garrett's dad's pack."

"Must have been rough."

"He never really got over what my mom did to him."

"Her leaving?"

"Not just that. When she left, she stole from the pack. Money. Each pack has central finances that everyone pays into, in case of emergencies, to pay for a safe house, that sort of thing. A small percentage, but it adds up. When my mom left, she took almost fifty grand."

"Whoa."

"Yeah. But that's not the worst. My dad was second in the pack. He was in charge of the finances. He was the reason she had access. So when she left..."

"He was blamed."

"We were in disgrace. Dad went from second in the pack to having his position in jeopardy. Everyone wanted to fight him. He was afraid for me, so we left and wandered around a while until we found a new pack. A good one in Phoenix— run by Garrett's dad. They welcomed us, but Dad never recovered. "

A new shifter has no rank, Tank had said.

"Didn't your dad have to fight for dominance again?"

"The pack he chose didn't make him fight for his place. But Dad didn't try to establish dominance. He took a low rank and didn't bother to fight. Almost like he stopped caring." Tank rubs his forehead. "Anyway. It was a long time ago."

"Parents." I shake my head. "Can't live with them, can't live without them."

"You can't replace family," Tank says softly.

Pain flashes through me.

"What was it like, being on your own with just your dad?"

"Stressful. Most lone wolves are outcasts. Packs try to run them out of their territory. I was only nine, but my dad made sure to teach me to shift, to fight. Even if we found a decent pack to join, he knew I'd need to be strong to fight to keep my place. Know the rules, that sort of thing."

"That explains a lot."

"What?"

"You're just so... rule abiding."

"Rules are important."

"So is having fun."

"Rules keep pack members safe. Wolves who don't follow them are ostracized."

I suck in a breath. Is that what he's afraid of, for me?

That I'll join a pack and be kicked out because of my fabulous Foxfire-ness?

"I'm sure you're a perfect pack citizen," I mutter. "A pillar of society."

"I wasn't when I first joined."

"Please." I sniff. "You've never made a faux pas in your life. Me, I'm a walking, talking faux pas."

"Yeah, you do that on purpose."

"What do you mean?" My chest is tight. I'm not sure where he's going with this.

He tugs a lock of my hair. "This screams *notice me*. But that's not what you want, is it?" He keeps playing with my hair. "In the wild, bright colors can mean poison. You dye your hair this wild to say *stay away, I'm a freak.*"

"Well, I am."

"No, you're not."

I shrug. "People are gonna think I'm weird. I may as well encourage it."

"You push people away."

"Oh, because you're so emotionally available? *I'm Tank.*" I mimic his deep voice and solemn look. *I eat trucks for breakfast. Why, no, I'm not a werewolf. I'll punish you if you say that again.* By the end, I'm giggling.

He shakes his head at me.

"I know you," I tease. "You can't hide from me."

"You don't need to hide from me, either," he says. Before I can ask him what he means, he calls, "Sunny, we're heading out."

11

F oxfire

BEFORE DUSK, we check into a hotel. Two rooms. One with a king, one with two double beds. I take my stuff and follow Sunny.

"I saw a lovely marketplace on the way in," Sunny prattles as we enter the room with the double beds. "I think I used to have a stall there, in the eighties. We should go down and see it. Do you think Tank will let us?"

"I think Tank needs his space." I set my bag down. "I was actually hoping to talk to you. Why didn't you tell me about Dad?"

"You never wanted to know."

"But... I'm like him. In a lot of ways."

"I know, dear. But Johnny was a free spirit. He'd want you to make your own way."

"I know. I have. I just want to know I'm not the only one like me. I want to be a part of something. A family."

"You are, Foxfire. You have me, and that tall drink of water who's probably wishing you were in his hotel room right now."

"Tank thinks I'm crazy."

Sunny just smiles.

"He's so different from me, Mom. It's weird. And yet..." It works. At least I think it does. He's done all this to help me.

"I like him."

"I'm so glad." I hide my eye roll as she hugs me.

"I'm so glad we had this chat." She heads off to the bathroom.

Maybe Mom's right. We make our own family, community. Maybe my dad will know some other foxes or Tank can hook me up. In any case, I have my mother. Maybe I should spend more time with her.

The bathroom door opens. Sunny walks out, blonde and pink hair wafting around her shoulders. She's stark naked. "Time for yoga," she trills.

"Um, you forgot your clothes."

"I always do sun salutation naked." She opens the curtains for the light to flood in and lays out a yoga mat. "After all, when we greet the sun, the rays burn away all artifice—"

"I'll just, uh... check on what Tank's friend found out about Johnny."

I scuttle for the door. My goal is to be out of there before she does downward facing dog.

Tank's room is a few doors down. Praying that a crowd doesn't gather to watch my mother do her *asanas* in the bare, I knock on the door.

"It's open," Tank says.

"How'd you know it was me?"

I step inside. Much darker. Tank probably isn't a sun salutation type dude. As my eyes adjust to the shadows, I realize he's sitting in a chair, huge body spilling out of it. He's got his shirt off, his hair damp like he toweled off. Water beads on his taut chest.

"I can smell you." He's got a paper bag in his hand, and he raises it to his lips. He must have gone out and gotten a bottle of something.

"Can you spare a sip of that?"

He offers it.

"Mom's doing her own version of hot yoga. Naked hot yoga. She has the blinds open."

Tank grimaces.

"Yeah," I agree and raise the bottle to take a swig. I cough a little as it sears my throat. I go to raise it again, but he takes it from me, pulls me into his lap.

I snuggle up to him. He rests his chin atop my head.

"Any luck on my dad's whereabouts?"

He shakes his head, and mine moves with it.

"Thanks again for all this. I owe you."

He rubs my back, slipping his hand under my shirt to toy with my bra strap. His cock grows against my leg.

"You've been taking care of me. It's time for me to take care of you." I slip to my knees between his legs.

He lets me pull down his jeans and put my mouth on him. I breathe in his scent, swallowing him down, making little begging noises, especially after he slips his fingers into my top and squeezes my breast. I dive down on his length, choking a little, and pop off, gasping.

He tugs me up before I can go again.

I wind my arms around his neck. He plunges his hand down my jeans.

"Fuck," he mutters like a prayer as his fingers encounter my slick folds. "No panties again? Bad girl." He finds my sweet spot and rubs it.

I rise to my tiptoes. In no time, I'm panting, sagging against his broad chest. I lick his neck, taste salt. My hand finds his dick and jacks slowly, but it's no use. I'm gonna blow.

Someone knocks on the door.

"Darling! What are our plans for dinner?"

I barely register her words until Tank whips his hand out of my pants.

"Uh, give us a few, Sunny," I call out. "We're naked."

Tank makes a disbelieving noise.

"All right, honey, I'll go down alone. Make sure you use protection!"

Tank heaves a sigh.

I giggle. "Come on." I tug him up. "Let's shower together."

~.~

Tank

I WRAP a towel around Foxfire and maneuver her out of the shower. She's flushed and dazed from the hard fucking I gave her up against the wall of the shower. I'm not sure her legs are steady, so I guide her to the bed and plunk her down.

It's getting both easier and harder being with her. I just

used up every last ounce of self-control being with her naked, fucking her without marking her. The entire time we were in that shower stall together, my fangs were out, ready to punch through her skin, leave my scent there so every other male can smell she's mine. Instead, I took it out on her pussy. I pounded that sweetness until she screamed herself hoarse. And already, I want round two of having those long legs wrapped around my waist, those fingernails digging into my back.

"What are we going to do for dinner?"

"I already ate."

She smacks me, giggling.

"Order whatever you want." I hand her a hotel room service menu.

"You sure?"

"Yeah, baby." I lie back and prop my arms behind my head, enjoying the sight of her with the towel falling open, her nipples chafed from my five o'clock shadow. She looks so happy, I don't care when she orders fifty dollars' worth of food and eats all of it. She prattles on and on about everything and nothing, and I don't care. I could stare at her for the rest of my life.

My phone vibrates, and I answer without checking it.

"Son?"

"Yes, sir." I straighten as if my father could see me, even though he's a few hundred miles away, in Phoenix. When we were lone wolves together, he ran our two person unit like a pack, so I was used to following an alpha. Technically, I'm now more dominant than he is, but old habits die hard.

"Just wanted to check on you, make sure everything's all right. My alpha heard from a human named Amber. She said Garrett's in trouble."

Fuck. "I'm not sure. Last I knew, Garrett was on his

way to Mexico." I hesitate, not sure how much Garrett wants other packs to know. Garrett's father is my father's alpha.

"To search for Sedona. That's what this Amber said."

"That's right." I pinch the bridge of my nose. "Look, call Trey or Jared, but if they don't answer, you'd better get down there. I haven't been able to reach them."

"My alpha's already on his way. I just wanted to see where you were in all this mess."

"I'm on another job."

"Tank, did you see my bra anywhere?" Foxfire shouts from the bathroom. "I can't find it."

Fuck. I hold the phone against my shirt until I'm outside the hotel room. "Garrett ordered me to go after a stray. Otherwise, I'd be down there already."

"That's... fine, son," my dad says.

I wince under the weight of his disapproval. "It's just a job. I should have things wrapped up soon. I was waiting to hear from Garrett, but if things have gone wrong—"

"No, no, you have to follow orders."

"I want to be there."

"You're second in the pack. Your alpha relies on you. Don't do anything to jeopardize that." *Especially not for a female.* He may as well come out and say it.

"Yes, sir."

He hangs up, and for a second I wonder if I should just pack everything up and hit the road for Mexico.

"Everything all right?" Foxfire chirps. She stands in the open door to the room, wearing a pair of skinny jeans and a tight T-shirt, head cocked to the side.

"Yeah, baby."

"You look like you got bad news."

Should I tell her what's going down with the pack? She'll

want to know, especially since it sounds like Amber's involved.

"I can cheer you up, big man." She comes to hug me.

"No." I fend her off. Foxfire stops in her tracks. She may play dense, but she's actually extremely sensitized to my moods, which makes me feel like an even bigger bastard. "This is pack business. I need to make a few calls. Why don't you go find your mother?"

Foxfire's smile is forced, her scent a confusing jumble. Women. So complicated. And now, my feelings are just as fucking complicated. My dad is right.

"Look," I try again, "a few people in the pack are in trouble. I don't mean—"

"No, it's all right." She picks up a hotel key and pockets it. "I'll go. Sunny wanted to visit the market. I'll go see what time it opens tomorrow—it'll be a good distraction for her while we search for Johnny."

"Okay. Thanks, baby."

A few more calls, and I'll mobilize the strongest in Garrett's pack to follow his dad down to Mexico. If I can't be there personally, at least I can help.

~.~

Foxfire

HE'S SHUTTING ME OUT. Again. Not that I had a right to be *in* in the first place. He's made it very clear: I'm not pack. Not that I care.

I wander around the empty market area, sniffing around the booths in a half-hearted attempt to find Sunny. I catch a whiff of something familiar, but I can't place it. The moon rises, and I head back, slowing my steps in case Tank is still talking to his pack. He doesn't want me to be a part of his world.

Maybe I'm meant to be alone, just me and my fox. I pause in a deserted alley and try to shift. But I can't. Not even staring at the moonlight.

Great. Now, even my fox has abandoned me.

Back at the hotel room, I knock, but no one's there. Tank must be out on an errand. I keep my jacket on and go out to lean on the balcony railing in the light of the moon.

So what if I'm alone? I'm used to it. But my fox wants to be around shifters. I can handle a group not wanting me, but this is the first time I've wanted to be a part of one. I hate it.

Stupid fox. Why couldn't I be a wolf?

"Foxfire?"

"I'm here," I call.

He comes and silently hugs me. He won't tell me what's wrong, but he holds me like he needs me.

"Everything all right?"

He grunts a non-answer.

"You know you can talk to me?"

He leans down and puts his mouth on mine. The kiss is long, and deep, and feels like an apology for something. I wish I knew what.

"Full moon tonight," I murmur.

"No, baby, it was last night."

I turn in his arms as he holds me.

"Do you think I'll ever be able to shift on my own?"

"Of course. It just takes practice."

"I don't." My voice wobbles. "I don't know if I can do it."

"Try it." He leads me back into the room.

"Okay." I strip off my clothes and take a deep breath, willing my body to morph.

"Relax, baby. This is natural. Just let her out."

This time, when I take a deep breath, the world changes immediately. I drop to four paws and yip at Tank.

"That's good, baby." He growls approval. His scent is a haven, strong and sure. But there's another one tickling my nose. I trot to the balcony and bark for him to follow.

"No, Foxfire." He starts toward me. "You should stay inside."

Before he can reach me, I rush out the door and leap from the balcony.

~.~

Tank

Foxfire disappears over the edge of the balcony. Her white tail streaks as she runs up the rise and disappears into the woods.

"Goddammit." I shuck my clothes and call my wolf. The world tilts as I turn. As soon as I right myself, I run after her. Her trail is red hot and easy to follow.

I keep to the shadows as she leads me into the heart of town. People might not notice a little fox, but they will definitely pay attention to a big wolf. Luckily, there aren't any cars.

I duck my head and lope across the concrete and hope

no one wants a wolf pelt in front of their fireplace. Regular bullets can't kill a werewolf, but they still hurt.

Damn you, little fox. My heart is rammed up in my throat, thinking of all the things that might go wrong out here, showing our animals in public. Someone's out there looking for Foxfire, and we're in a town where there might be shifters. She isn't safe running around in fox form.

She leads me to the marketplace, abandoned for the night. When I catch up, she's sniffing around one of the booths.

I bark at her. She automatically crouches, ducking her head. Her fox knows submission, even if my beautiful girl sometimes fights it.

I trot toward her, and the scent hits me, surrounding me. Fox. And not Foxfire—but another shifter. A fox shifter has been here, in this booth.

Foxfire faces me, her ears standing up and her tail wagging.

See? she seems to say.

I jerk my head toward the hotel. *Head back.* She doesn't protest. We lope back together, my larger body casting a shadow over her smaller one. Two animals might attract attention, but not as much as two naked humans. Luckily, there's a little hill under our second-story room, and no one else is on the balcony. With a running jump, I reach the railing and clear it. I turn and wait for the little fox to come. Her leap isn't as high, and I catch her by the scruff of the neck. I carry her in like this and set her down, fixing her with another glare.

She's not afraid of me at all. Of course not, my wolf points out. She's our mate.

I shift first, grunting with the force and speed of the change. I stride to the balcony door and close it.

"Change, Foxfire. Now."

She does and curls up for a moment, shivering. Shifting is still hard for her. "Did you smell it?" she says as soon as she can catch her breath. "There's someone like me. Another fox."

"That's good, baby. You did good." I kneel to tip some water into her mouth, holding the bottle until she can sit up. It doesn't take as long as the last time. She's getting stronger. My wolf approves.

"Do we have any more steak?" she asks.

I pull out the last one left over from room service from the mini-fridge, sit on the bed and pat my lap. She curls up, and I feed her. It's a simple act, but it deeply satisfies my wolf. When she's finished eating, I make her drink the rest of the water. I hold her the whole time. Fits right in my arms like she was made for me.

"Feeling better?"

"Yeah. Tomorrow we can track the shifter, right?"

"Yes. But we do it my way. Less chance of getting buck-shot in our ass." Stern tone.

She squirms like it excites her to be in trouble. "Yes."

I cage her throat in my hand without applying any pressure. "You know what naughty foxes get?"

"Punishment?" Her pulse hammers against my palm. No fear in her scent. Just anticipation. And arousal.

I slip my hand between her legs and brush the pad of my middle finger over her clit. She throws her head back over my shoulder, arching her breasts toward my mouth. She's so fucking responsive.

I've never met another female—human or shifter—whose body is so clearly mine to command. Foxfire—the crazy hippie child—turns into a certifiable porn star every time we touch. Ready and willing to take anything I give her, no matter how rough. Willing to serve, too. I've never had a female so generous with her mouth on my cock before.

"Get up on your hands and knees, baby," I direct.

She scrambles to obey, wagging her beautiful ass in my face. I stand up beside the bed and arrange her hips in my direction, letting a slap fall on one cheek.

"Is this what you wanted?" I squeeze her bare cheek and deliver another smack.

"Yes." Her breath leaves in a gust.

"You sure?"

"Yes, please," she whispers, not quite a plea.

I hardly recognize the growl coming from my mouth. I slip my digits between her legs, again, stroke her slick folds. "You're wet."

"Well, yeah. You're naked."

"Naughty little fox." My hand claps her bottom and strokes her slit again.

"Yes." She wriggles as I tease her sweet spot, her fingers clawing at the covers.

I keep her on the edge, alternating light smacks with frigging her clit until she's moaning with need. I want to plow into her, fuck her until tomorrow, but my wolf is right below the surface. The full moon was last night, so the urge to mark her shouldn't be getting stronger, but it is.

I pick up her hips and flip her around to face me. "Suck me," I order roughly because I need relief, or I'm going to do something I regret.

She parts those sexy lips and engulfs my cock with her hot mouth. "That's it, baby."

She goes to town on me, trying to swallow me down deep, driving me crazy.

I let out a curse.

She pops off and nips my thigh, teeth sharp as a fox's. Her animal is right at the edge, too.

I roar, my wolf mad to mark her, to dominate my little fox and show her which one of us does the biting.

She kneels up, licking her glossy lips. "Oops. Sorry." Her mock innocence is too much for my self-control. To keep myself from taking her, I push her down on her belly with a hand at her nape and smack her wriggling ass.

She writhes, not really trying to escape. "Spank me, Tank. Harder."

Oh, fuck no. Did she really say that?

I warm her ass, slapping harder, loving the way she bucks on the bed, the little grunts and whimpers she makes.

The next time I check between her legs, I groan. "Fuck, baby, you're sopping wet."

"Tank," she screams as her orgasm hits her. She squeezes her thighs around my fingers. I wedge three into her pussy and plunge as her muscles contract and spasm.

I lie down beside her and pull her into my arms, trying to slow my breath, then push the wolf back down.

She rolls into me, pressing against my bare chest. She nuzzles my skin, and I breathe in her intoxicating scent.

She licks my neck, but I don't think she's aware of it; her fox is still close to the surface. After a moment, she raises her head.

"Sorry."

"It's okay, baby. Do what you want."

She explores, tracing the curves of muscles, finding every little scar where a wolf's teeth or claws caught me when I was a teen and didn't have enough to eat, so my body didn't fully heal.

She runs her tongue over one flat nipple, and I shiver.

She kisses down my chest and slowly arranges herself on her knees, between my thighs.

My dick bobs with approval, but I say, "You think you deserve my cock?"

She nods.

I catch her hair and tug it so she looks up at me. "You gonna be a good girl?"

"Maybe. Probably."

"Fuck," I whisper. This girl drives me fucking insane.

I burrow my fingers in her hair, watching the rainbow of colors and waves cascade as she hollows her cheeks and sucks.

My vision starts to tunnel, hips strain to push my cock farther into her mouth. I don't want to choke her, at least that's what I tell myself when I tug her up on all fours, positioning myself behind her.

I even remember a condom, which is a goddamn miracle.

She waits for me, pussy slick and ready, thighs trembling with my desire. I slide right in.

I'm not a big talker. But there are words exploding in my head. The ones I'm showing her with each hard thrust: *I own you. You are mine.*

I pound into her. She presses her front into the bed and pushes back against me, meeting me, welcoming me. I hold her down and hammer her reddened ass.

"Yes, Tank, yes!" Her tight muscles grip my dick.

I flip her over, prop her leg over my shoulder and pound myself home.

"Oh, I'm going to—"

"Take it, baby." I palm and squeeze her ass.

A cry breaks from her as her orgasm blows up.

I lose my mind the second she starts keening. Every inch, every limb, every cell vibrates with white hot pleasure.

"Fuck." I fall on top of her, my arms holding my weight but my body covering hers.

I tuck my face into her neck and shoulder. My teeth scrape her skin, and she shudders, still in the grip of her ecstasy.

I hammer into her, blind with need. My balls tighten, thighs grip. My thrusts become erratic.

"Fuck, yes, Foxfire!" I shout as I come. As I let loose, I bite down. Hard.

Hard enough to break the skin. A mating bite.

I fucking marked her.

12

F *oxfire*

I BOUNCE up at the crack of dawn. Tank slumbers beside me, and I let him. He probably needs a break, poor guy.

My fox is eager to be on the prowl.

I check the mirror before I leave. Yep, Tank clearly bit me. It's deeper than I first thought. Broke the skin and everything, but it's already healed. I push my hair back to admire the bite and then arrange my colorful locks over the marks to hide them.

I stop by my mom's room on the way out, pressing my ear against her door. I try my nose, but I only smell hotel carpet and cleaner. My fox is impatient, so I hurry on down to the market. It's early, and most of the stalls are being set up. To my surprise, Sunny is there, holding a paper cup. Tea, from the smell of it. My nose is getting better.

"Darling! Did you have fun last night?

"Yeah. It was wild," I report, truthfully enough. I didn't check before I left, but I'd guess last night's shenanigans broke the bed again.

"Good." She beams. "You're up early."

"Uh, yeah. There's a booth I want to see. Where did you get that?" I motion to her cup.

"The coffee shop—want one?"

"Yeah, if you don't mind. I was going to sniff—uh, check out some of these booths." I hand her my money and stroll on.

The booth I care about is already set up, the table sparsely dotted with products. Wood carvings. Woven blankets. Jars of honey. That sort of thing.

Then the fox comes into view. She wears a long jean skirt and flower-patterned blouse, homemade from the look of it.

As soon as I come close, she stiffens.

"Hey," I call, keeping my distance. "Can I talk to you?"

Her nostrils flare. She's caught my scent.

"I'm just here to talk." I spread my hands.

I pad closer and pick up a jar of honey, pretending to study it. Red Farm Honey, the label reads.

"All right," she says softly. "But in a second, I gotta go."

I study her. According to Tank, there are few fox shifters. Is it possible we're related?

"I'm looking for information about... someone my mom knew." I point out Sunny, who's chatting with someone outside the coffee shop. "She does markets, too, and had a booth like this next to someone. His name was Johnny."

Recognition flashes in her eyes. "I'm sorry. I can't tell you anything."

I just stare at her.

"I don't know anything about that." She glances around

nervously, as if she's expecting someone to pop out and attack her. "I have to go." She darts around the stall and gets on a bike she yanks out from under her table.

"Hey, wait," I say. "Please. Johnny was my father."

She pauses. For a moment, I think she's gonna talk to me.

"Foxfire," Tank's voice rings out over the market.

The blood drains from the woman's face. "Wolf," she mouths.

"No, please," I call as I watch my only link to my father ride out of town as if escaping a fire.

"Who was that?" Tank rumbles behind me. I whirl, and he must read the desperation on my face. "Was that her?" I nod, and he grabs my hand. "Come on." I let him pull me along to the hotel parking lot. "She's on a bike," he tells me as we climb into Daisy. "If she comes this way often, I can track her."

We pull into traffic just in time for me to see Sunny crossing the street toward us, two paper cups in her hand.

~.~

"THERE'S ONLY one road she could've taken," Tank says after I point out the way the fox shifter went. We left Sunny at the market, telling her we'd be back soon.

We ride in tense silence, quickly leaving all buildings behind for an open desert. When we get out of town, Tank pulls over. "I'm going on all fours now. Follow me in the car. If anyone sees me and asks questions, you tell them I'm a wolfhound crossed with a European mountain dog and whistle for me. I'll come when you call."

The thought of Tank acting domesticated doesn't even make me smile.

Tank ducks in the back to strip off his clothes. Within a minute, a huge wolf leaps out and trots along the highway.

I grip the steering wheel and inch behind him.

The fox shifter looked so frightened. Is she really one of my people? What does she know about my father? Are all fox shifters that skittish?

A few cars pass, but no one stops. Tank leads me onto a small turnoff and disappears for a moment behind the rocks. Then he sticks his head out and barks. I turn off the car, grab his stuff, and lock it.

Tank strides out in human form and pulls on his clothes. "Trail goes this way. You want to do this? We can head back to town and wait for my contact to see what she dug up on your dad."

"No," I say, remembering the woman's face in the market when I mentioned Johnny's name. She knew him. She was just frightened. "This is the hottest lead we have. Let's go."

We hike along. The reddish orange rocks would make the perfect camouflage for a fox.

"As soon as she scented you were a wolf, she ran," I comment. "Do you think she's a loner?"

"I've heard that weaker shifters stick together. They're secretive, and there's strength in numbers. I don't know any foxes, though. Either because there aren't many, or because they don't make their presence widely known."

"Or because we don't want a stinking wolf trespassing on our land." A voice rings out, and I start, looking for the voice. A giant pile of red rocks blocks our way, but there's no sign of anyone. I step forward, and Tank puts his hand out to stop me.

"Take your hands off her, wolf," someone snarls. About fifteen men appear from behind the rocks. Some of them rise from the brush behind us. They all have shotguns, and they're all pointed at Tank.

We're surrounded.

"Stay where you are, wolf."

Tank throws up his hands.

"No, don't shoot." I raise my hands also. "We mean no harm." To Tank, I whisper, "Did you smell them?"

"No."

"This whole place smells like fox, boy." The oldest-looking fox, a sandy-haired man with a seamy face says, hands on his slender hips.

More men surround us. They're sunburnt, short and muscular. They all look familiar. Several are identical from the reddish hair to the dirty overalls.

"We're not armed," Tank says.

"A wolf is a weapon. He doesn't need one."

"Look, he won't hurt you," I blurt. "He's just helping me find my kin."

The man narrows his eyes at me. "Who are you?"

"I'm Johnny's daughter."

"Johnny?" He stares at me, as if trying to figure out how I'd look without rainbow-colored hair.

"Probably lying, Pa," one of the younger foxes says. He's a spitting image of the older leader. Tank stirs at my side. If anyone threatens me, he might snap. They'll hurt him.

"Jordy," the leader barks, and another fox appears, a woman. She keeps her head bowed and shoulders hunched, but she's the one I saw in the marketplace. "This her?"

Jordy nods.

One of the men steps closer to me and sniffs. "She smells like wolf." He spits on the ground.

Tank shifts beside me, and the shotguns snaps to readiness.

"No, no, this isn't what we want," I say. "I'm here because I'm looking for my father. I've never met him, but he kept in touch with my mother. She's human. But I'm a fox. See?" I raise my hand and will it to change. Maybe because I'm desperate, or maybe because my fox knows she's around her own kind, my hand turns to a paw with reddish fur.

A murmur ripples around the group.

"You'd better come with us," the leader says. "It's not safe to talk out in the open like this."

"What? Why?" I ask, but the foxes are already melting away. Pa nods at Jordy, and she comes to stand beside me. "Because"—her voice is practically a whisper—"the drones. They might be watching."

~.~

THE FOXES MARCH us to the hills and lead us into one of the caves honeycombed into the reddish brown rock. They pause to argue whether to blindfold Tank before one points out that with his sense of smell, he could find them anyway.

"I mean you no harm," Tank says. "I'm here to help Foxfire."

"I'll be dead before I believe the word of a wolf," one of the younger men says and spits.

"Now, Jason," Pa cautions.

The shotguns relax, but Tank hovers close to me. The only one who's not openly hostile is Jordy.

"Sit here," she whispers when we're sheltered in the mouth of the cave. The foxes gather around us, their leaders taking places on a few rocks that help them stand a head over Tank.

They pass around a jug of something that smells like Tank's bottle in a brown paper bag, only a hundred times stronger. They don't offer it to us.

"Is this how you treat all your visitors?" Tank eyes the guns.

"We don't get many visitors," Jason says. The fox next to him, almost identical down to his work boots and dirty overalls, spits.

"Why have you come?" Pa asks.

"I just want to find my father. Can you tell me about Johnny?"

"Yeah, he was one of us," Jason speaks up. "My dumb brother."

"So, we're related?"

"All fox shifters are related," my uncle answers. "There aren't many of us. No thanks to the wolves."

"My pack never did anyone harm," Tanks says.

"You didn't have to. Shifters disappearing all over, and it's got the stink of wolf all over it." Jason glares at us.

"What are you talking about?" I ask.

"Johnny's gone," Pa says bluntly. "He disappeared a year ago."

Tank and I exchange glances. I notice Jordy staring hard at the ground.

"What, he just disappeared? Did you go looking for him?"

"No. Didn't have to. The wolves took him. Jeb and Joey

went and sniffed them out." My uncle points to two other sandy-haired shifters who look so much alike, they could be brothers. Or cousins.

"Maybe you should ask your wolf where your father is," Pa says.

"Wolves aren't taking people." Tank frowns.

"Says a wolf," Jason sneers.

"Do you know where they took him?" I interrupt their glaring contest.

"I just know they took him. Snatched him from the market last summer," Jeb or Joey answers. All these J names and similar faces, it's hard to tell them apart.

"Johnny ran the market stall before Jordy. Had all these high falutin' ideas of foxes being part of society," Pa says.

"See where it got him," Jason mutters.

I swallow around the knot in my throat.

"Now, Jordy runs the stall. We didn't want it, but she insisted."

Jordy visibly pales. She hasn't lifted her eyes from the ground. It's hard to see her standing up for anything.

"And look what happened," Pa continues berating Jordy. "A wolf tracked us."

"It's not her fault," I say. "I just found out I'm a shifter. My fox wanted to find its kin." I look around at the shadowed faces.

"You live alone, girl?" Jason looks me up and down.

"She's under my protection." Tank moves closer to me.

A few foxes shake their heads.

"Please, can you tell me anything else about my father?"

"Johnny was an odd one. Moved around a bit, even took up residence in town at one time. Moved back here when shifters started disappearing."

"What sort of shifters?" Tank asks.

"Grizzlies, foxes, eagles. A few big cats. Mostly the loners, or the weak."

"Who would be taking them?" I ask.

"We don't know. Wolves, some of them."

"Not my pack," Tank says quickly.

"Does it matter? You're all the same." Angry mutters ripple around us, and the shotguns bristle again.

"And Johnny, did he know this was happening?" I step in front of Tank, hoping to keep my kin from turning into a mob.

"He knew," Pa answers. "And he wanted to stop it. Didn't back off until too late. They got his scent, and when he went out to market, they took him."

"Kin keep to kin," Jason says, and a few foxes repeat his words in an eerie chant. My extended family feels more cult-like by the second. "Foxes are meant to live in secret," my uncle continues. "Johnny never learned. And now he's gone."

13

F *oxfire*

IT'S late afternoon when we hike back to Daisy. The foxes provide an escort to the edge of their land, but only Jordy walks with us.

"Hey," I whisper to her as we go single file through a dense thicket. "You're not in trouble, are you? I mean, it's not your fault we found you. We would've sniffed you out one way or another."

She shakes her head, but I don't quite believe her.

When we hear the sound of cars on the highway, Tank and I find ourselves alone.

"You all right?" he asks as we climb into Daisy.

I barely nod. My father is missing and has been for most of the year. My kin are a bunch of backwoods, inbred, wolf-hating hillbillies. We didn't see any females other than Jordy, but if she's their example of a liberated woman, I don't even want to know what they think of hippie feminists who dye their hair and own businesses. No wonder Johnny didn't bring my mother into the fold. As much as she might dig the homemade clothes and living in caves, she couldn't give up coffee shops and modern plumbing.

"Foxfire?" Tank has pulled over. We're at a diner on the edge of town.

"We should call Sunny," I say. My mom might be worried. Or, knowing her, assume we snuck off to make love in the woods all day. I pull my phone out and shoot her a text, asking if we can bring her dinner. She replies right away that she made friends with a few local market people and is going to a vegan potluck and meditation session with them tonight.

Tank guides me into the diner and orders food. When it comes, I pick at it.

After polishing off his huge order, Tank bumps my foot. "So, you met your kin. Pretty smart of them to hide out like that."

"Did you know there were... people... living like that?"

"No. But I'm not surprised. It's dangerous for the weaker species. They lie low." He frowns. "You gonna eat the rest of your burger?"

I shake my head.

"What do they do if they have to go to the doctor?"

"Shifters don't need much medical care."

"What about food? Schools?"

"They don't trust any outsiders. They take care of their own."

He signals to the waitress and asks her to box my food up, along with a few extra orders.

Halfway to the car, he stops and pulls me alongside the

building. He crowds me against the wall and frames my face with his big hands. "Foxfire, talk to me."

"They didn't know he had a daughter," I say around the lump in my throat. "They had no idea..."

Tank searches my face.

"He didn't want me." My voice wobbles.

"Baby." He hugs me. "You know that's not true. He sent your mom money all these years."

"Why didn't he ever come to meet me?"

"He thought you were human, remember? Maybe he wanted to protect you."

"Yeah."

"Do you think he wanted to expose you to those people? Risk their laying claim to you, demanding you be raised among them?"

I shake my head. Life with Sunny was definitely better than with the extras from the cast of *Deliverance*.

"Sounds like he was trying to escape them himself."

"But what about what they said?" I ask. "Shifters disappearing?"

Tank straightens. Shadows move across his face. "I don't know," he says finally. "I can't say whether their claims are true or not. Your father could've just run and escaped them. We may never find out."

"It just sucks. I finally have a reason to seek out my father, and I'm a year too late."

"I know, baby. I know."

I head into the diner for a pit stop while Tank loads the food into Daisy. When I return, a soft voice calls my name.

I whirl and peer into the shadows. "Jordy?"

My female fox kin inches away from the wall where her bike leans.

"You came to find me?"

"I wanted to give this to you." She holds out a small brown object, a wallet. "It's Johnny's. He left it hidden at the market stall the day he disappeared. I found it in the locked money box. I was the only one who had a key."

I flip the worn leather open and peer at the driver's license. A solemn-faced man, light-haired, with freckles, looks up at me.

"Johnny," she confirms. "He was my brother. Older by a bunch of years."

I close the wallet, hiding my father's picture away. "That makes you my aunt."

"Yeah." She smiles shyly. She doesn't look that much older than me, maybe five years.

"Foxfire," Tank calls. Jordy startles.

"It's okay." I step into the light and wave at Tank to wait a minute. Jordy cringes against the wall, the whites of her eyes flashing in the dark. "He doesn't bite, I promise."

"Wolves are so dangerous," Jordy whispers.

"You get used to him." I shrug.

She shakes her head. "The clan doesn't want him around, even if he is your mate."

"My what?"

"He marked you." She jerks her chin at my neck. I put a hand over the place where Tank bit me. "That's what wolves do when they find their mates."

"So?" I say, not certain what she means by *mate*. "I'm still one of you."

"No, you ain't. And that's the way it's gotta be."

"But you're my family."

"You'd better just forget all of us. Johnny would want you to. Johnny wished he could sometimes."

"Everything all right?" Tank walks slowly toward us.

"I gotta go." Jordy grabs her bike and climbs on, poised

to flee.

"You going to be okay?" Tank asks her.

"Yeah."

I add, "You're not in trouble for coming to talk to us?"

"I had to come. Johnny would've wanted it."

"Jordy..." I want to tell her she doesn't have to go back, that she can come and live with me. But I don't even know what I'm going to do. I thought I'd find my father and things would magically make sense.

"Write down our numbers," Tank decides for me. I fumble in my purse for a pen and paper and take down the digits. "You get in trouble, you call." He holds the paper out to Jordy. "We'll get you out."

She snatches the paper and folds it so it disappears among her clothes before pedaling away.

"You okay, baby?" His hand rests on my neck, stroking.

"Yeah," I whisper, watching the lone figure ride into the wilderness.

~.~

Tank

FOXFIRE'S quiet as I drive to the hotel. Jordy gave her something. I can smell it in her purse, but she doesn't mention it, so I don't bring it up.

Back in the room, she disappears for a few minutes in the bathroom. I give her space, touching her lightly when she leaves, and I take my turn to wash up.

When I come out, she's lying on the bed, staring at the ceiling. The bag of food sits by her, untouched. I don't like how little she's eaten, but I understand. It's been an intense day.

I lie down beside her.

"What do you need?"

A little sigh escapes her. Her scent changes. Before I can analyze it, she rolls to face me, blinking her large gray eyes.

"Make love to me, Tank."

I don't know what to say, so I stay silent. Her whole world is upside down. I'm the only one she has to talk to. I'm happy to be there for her, I'm just not sure I deserve her trust.

"Please." She wriggles closer, her head tilting up to mine. "I need to be touched." She lifts her hand, hesitates, and then touches my hair. "I need you."

I swallow, hard. I thought resisting Foxfire, the crazy-haired sex kitten, was hard, but seeing her hurting guts me. Nothing on the planet would keep me from giving my mate what she needs. Even if I haven't wrapped my brain around the fact that I've marked her.

As in, she's mine forever. And I'm still not sure that's the best idea.

What am I saying? My wolf fucking loves the idea. I just have this itchy feeling about how this will all fall out with the pack. I'm up here in Flag when I should be keeping an eye on Eclipse and Garrett's businesses in Tucson. Have I forsaken my pack for a female, just like my father did?

But I can figure that out later. Right now, my babygirl needs me. I wrap my hand around her nape, pull her close, and kiss her.

We don't talk. We don't have to.

I'm not rough this time. I give it to her sweet. Not quite

tender—I don't know if that's possible for me—but as gentle as I can. I stroke my tongue into her mouth, suck at her lips. Pull her shirt off and drag down the straps of her bra. I worship her nipples, sucking, pinching, kissing. I move down her belly, divest her of her pants.

She starts begging for my cock the minute my mouth is on her core, and I don't have the heart to delay her orgasm. I stand up and yank off my clothes.

"You want this, baby?" I grip my cock.

"Yes, Tank. I need you."

I climb over her and rub my cock along her glossy slit. For once I use some restraint, inching in slowly, doing my best not to turn this into another bed-breaking slam fest.

She arches and squeezes me tight.

Fuck. Maybe it will be another bed-breaker. I rock into her, holding her gray gaze, lacing my fingers over the tops of hers.

"Is this what you need, little fox?"

"Yeah," she chokes. She's popping her pelvis up to meet me on every stroke, rubbing her sweet spot over my cock. "Yes!"

I keep our bodies connected but roll over. Let her drive, for once. She straddles me, and I grip her hips, sliding her up and down the length of my cock. Her breasts bounce, color flushes her cheeks. She drops her hands to my chest and digs her nails into my skin. I let her take over the rhythm.

Her eyes glaze, lips part. She's already shot to outer space, but I don't make her stay with me. She needs this. "Take it, baby. Take what you need."

She rides me fast, making the sexiest little grunts until she comes. I hold her hips in place and jack mine up, fucking her deep until I go off like a firecracker.

She hums and settles on top of me, naked, her cheek cradled on my chest. I run my hand up and down her back, soothing her, listening to her heartbeat slow.

"Whatcha thinking about?" I nudge her.

"My kin."

"Ah."

Yeah, there are no words.

"At least I found them." It's an obvious attempt at a silver lining, and it makes my chest tighten for her. "And I guess we know why I'm such a freak."

"Don't do that," I say immediately.

"Do what?" She raises her head.

"*Nobody* calls you a freak. If I catch anyone calling you names, I'll make them pay." I waggle my eyebrows. "Even if it's you."

Her lips quirk with a reluctant grin. "You're going to spank me for calling myself names?"

"Yes."

She snorts, but I let her see I'm 100 percent serious. Not about punishing her, but about defending her. Because despite my father's advice, I will choose Foxfire over the pack if it comes to it. Any one of my pack brothers judges her, and they're going to swallow my fist whole.

I roll on top of her, holding most of my weight while still covering her slender body with mine. She doesn't move, doesn't breathe, looking up at me like I hung the fucking moon. I want to bottle this feeling forever. The glory of being her lover, her protector.

"No one insults my baby." I nuzzle her neck, right over the mark I gave her. I haven't explained it to her yet. I still had to wrap my own mind around it, and she has way too much on hers. But I will.

She's mine now, whether she likes it or not.

14

F *oxfire*

SOMEONE KNOCKS ON THE DOOR. Tank and I are in a tangle of limbs.

"Go-way," I mumble.

"It's okay, baby. I got it," Tank whispers, the ghost of his fingers trailing down my back as he leaves the bed.

My mother's voice mingles with dreams of returning to the fox caves to meet my father and convincing Jordy to dye her hair blue.

I jerk as Tank's warm hand covers my shoulder.

"Foxfire, we've got a problem."

I come awake. "What?"

"Someone slashed our tires last night. Your mom was out early this morning and found it."

"Oh no."

"The vandals didn't leave a note or a anything, but the tires stink of fox piss."

I start to get up, and Tank presses my back. "You stay. I'll handle it. I saw a shop right around the corner."

"Why would the foxes do this?"

"Send a message. They don't want us visiting again."

"By making it hard for us to leave?"

"They may not be the smartest shifters out there. Your father must've been the exception."

"I'm sorry."

"Not your fault. Rest, baby. You need sleep."

He's not wrong. The second he's gone, I'm falling back into my crazy, jumbled dreams.

When I finally get up, Tank isn't back yet, so I shower and do my morning stuff. There are dark circles under my eyes, and I look like I've lost weight. Even my normally brilliant plumage droops a little. Maybe I should become a redhead. Or blue—maybe my dream was a sign.

My father's wallet lies on the bedside table, where I put it last night.

I open it.

"Hey," I tell my dad. "Look, Sunny says I didn't want to know you when I was growing up. That's not true. I wanted to know why the other kids had dads and I didn't. I wanted to meet you. But whenever she brought it up, she's right, I denied it.

"Sunny did her best. I know you did, too. But I wish you had been more selfish. I was a tough kid. I could've handled it. I wish I had known you. I have a feeling now I never will."

I flip the wallet closed. Why did my dad leave his wallet before he skipped town? Was it a message to Jordy?

I search through, and other than a few folded bills,

change and a library card, there's nothing of note. Except when I search an inner pocket, I discover a brass key. A small piece of tape marks it with a long number. A code? Is this a key to a safe? I tuck the key back carefully. Tank will know. I grab my phone and dial him.

A few rings later, I realize his bag is vibrating. He must've left his phone here. I go get it, ready to run down and find Tank and tell him what I discovered. He has a few missed calls from last night and this morning. One's from Garrett. There's even a text from a "Jared." "U alive?!?"

Guess Tank has been neglecting his pack to deal with my drama.

As I stand there, holding the phone and feeling guilty, it rings. The caller's name is "Dad".

Biting my lip, I answer, "Tank's phone. He's not here right now, but I can take a message."

"Who's this?" an older version of Tank's voice asks.

"I'm Foxfire. Did you want to speak to Tank? He left his phone here but should be back—"

"Is there a reason you're answering his phone?"

"He just ran out on an errand and left it here. I'll tell him to call his pack as soon as he gets back—he's been busy... um... helping me with some family problems."

Silence. I wince. This is not how I wanted an introduction with Tank's dad to go.

"I'm a fox shifter," I offer, then wonder if it was wise to tell him that. "You're his father? It's nice to meet you—"

"Look," the man interrupts. "I don't know who you are, and I don't care. Tank has been off with you while his alpha and members of pack were in trouble."

"What?" The air sucks out of the room.

"I don't know what he's doing with you, but his alpha's

back in town now and wants answers. Tank needs to wise up and get back to his duties."

It's my turn to be silent.

"Listen, I don't mean to be hard on you. But Tank's second in the pack. You know what that means? His alpha relies on him. He doesn't need a woman messing up his place in the pack."

"I wouldn't do that." I will my voice not to shake. "We only just met, but I care about your son."

"If you care for him, you'll be careful with him. You say you're a fox shifter?"

"Y-yes."

"Shifters don't mix with other species. Tank needs a mate who understands him. He belongs with his kind."

"I'll tell Tank you called," I whisper and hang up. My body is numb, like I've been slammed into the ground.

Shifters don't mix with other species.

My kin, waving guns at Tank.

Tank needs a mate who understands him.

Tank at the wheel of his truck, trying to explain how a pack works to me.

He belongs with his kind.

Tank's face, filled with pity as he looks at Jordy. At me.

The missed calls. His insistence he can't involve his pack. His father's ugly words, not angry, but worried.

I don't belong in his world. He definitely doesn't belong in mine. I'm doing just what his mother did, putting his good pack standing in jeopardy.

Selfish, selfish, selfish. I pack up my stuff and put it in Sunny's room.

I find out from Sunny where Tank had the car towed. Turns out, it's a short walk from the hotel.

Tank comes around the bus as I approach, rubbing his greasy hands on a rag.

"Tires should be here by noon. I just did an oil change, and I'm going to check a few more things before we go." He glances at me. "Everything okay?"

My feet falter. I rehearsed what I'm going to say on the way over, but at the sight of him, biceps stretching the sleeves of his shirt, jeans creased with oil stains, proof that he was taking care of my mom's vehicle even though we didn't ask, and she probably can't pay. Tank being Tank.

"So, we're leaving?"

He shrugs. "It's up to you. I was thinking we'd stay a few more days, see if we can get any more leads on your dad—"

I shake my head. It's just like his dad said. I'm a ball and chain, dragging him down.

"You need to go," I blurt. His head jerks back, brows knotting. "I mean... I think it's best if you go back to your pack. They need you. My kin won't talk to me with you around and..." I shrug.

He studies me a moment. "What's wrong, Foxfire?"

I take a deep breath and bring out the big guns.

"When were you going to tell me you marked me as your mate?"

~.~

Tank

. . .

FOXFIRE rubs her palms on her jeans but stands her ground. Her scent is off somehow, and she isn't looking me directly in the eyes.

Until now.

"Well? You marked me, Tank."

Fuck. "Who told you that?"

"Jordy." She pulls her hair to the side, baring the red weal. It's healed up nicely. Shifters heal fast, but the serum in my fangs for claiming a mate makes sure it leaves a mark.

"Foxfire—"

"Why, Tank?" Her voice is hard. I've never heard this tone from her before. If I didn't know any better, I'd say someone abducted my woman and put an actor in her place.

"I messed up," I say, rubbing the back of my neck. "I didn't mean to."

She closes her eyes.

Fuck.

"Explain."

"I can't. My wolf wants you. He's always wanted you. But it was wrong of me to do it. I should've had better control."

"We don't belong," she says. "You're a wolf, and I'm a fox."

I start toward her, and she puts her hand out to keep space between us.

"Your dad called."

I can't keep up with the change of subject. I realize she's holding out my cell phone.

"Garrett and the others are wondering where you are. Your pack has been in some trouble."

"What are you talking about?"

"They need you, Tank." She takes a deep breath. "I don't need you. Not anymore."

I search her face. Nothing of Foxfire in there, no light, no excitement. Stony and cold. I marked her without permission. She has a right to be upset.

As soon as I take my cell phone, she turns away. She's right. My phone is blown up with texts and calls from the pack. My alpha. My dad.

"I took a call from your dad," she says. "I shouldn't have done it, but you left your phone, and I didn't want them worrying. Anyway, he told me your pack needs you."

Fuck. There's a text from Garrett to the entire pack. A meeting, tonight. "I should go."

"I think it's for the best." She doesn't look back at me. "We can give you a ride—"

Dammit. Leaving her—especially now, when she's pissed at me—goes against every cell in my body—shifter or human. But I can't shirk my duties to the pack, and she clearly doesn't want me here. Maybe she just needs some space. I'll reconnect with her after the pack meeting and get her to talk to me.

"The car shop has a motorcycle I can buy and take back to Tucson. The repairs are all paid for, and the tires should be on before closing. I'll call when I get to Tucson to make sure you and your mom are all set."

"We'll be fine," she says tightly. "No need to check on us."

Fuck a goddamn duck. I guess I'm getting a taste of my own goddamn medicine. She's totally shut me out.

My instincts scream at me not to go, but staying doesn't make sense. The long motorcycle ride will clear my head. So will reconnecting with my pack.

~.~

FOXFIRE

I WANDER THROUGH THE MARKET, stopping at my dad's old booth. The scent of fox is fading. Something tells me Jordy won't be back to run the booth. This is a dead end. This whole trip was.

I choke back a sob. The wind picks up. Old newspapers swirl in the flurries. A gust carries the scent of patchouli oil to me.

"Foxfire?" Sunny approaches. "I just saw Tank—he bought a used motorcycle from the repair shop and is heading back to Tucson. Is everything all right?"

I burst into tears.

~.~

BACK IN OUR HOTEL ROOM, I tell her everything. Everything except about us being shifters, of course. She grimaces at my description of Johnny's family but doesn't seem surprised.

"He told me a little about them. Enough to make it clear I'd never want to meet them. Everyone worked in the family business, with no outside pursuits. The men were domineering, the women shut-ins. Very rigid society, very patriarchal. Your father wasn't that way at all."

I show her the wallet, and she smiles at the picture of Johnny.

"I found this." I pull out the key. "I'm not sure what it

opens, but he left it behind when he disappeared." Or was taken. I don't know much about shifter society, but if his clan thought he was abducted, I believed them. After all, he'd wandered off before, when he met my mother. This sounded different.

"This probably opens a safety deposit box," Sunny muses. "Everything he sent me was from the post office here. I already went to visit—very nice people. They remember Johnny."

"Have they seen him?"

"Not since early last year."

As I take the key back, I can't shake the feeling of dread. My father disappeared and left his wallet in a lockbox. Maybe he meant to return and put it there for safekeeping. Or maybe not.

"S-should we..." I stumble over the words because they feel like an acknowledgment Johnny is really gone. For good. "Should we go see what it opens?"

"I think your father left it for someone to find."

~.~

PAPERS, papers, and more papers—everything from handwritten notes to photocopied newspaper clippings. My father wasn't a fox, he was a packrat.

Hiding my disappointment from Sunny, I dump the contents into a box the nice post office people provide and return to the hotel. We spread everything out on the bed, and I eat my leftovers from last night as Sunny sifts through it.

"Interesting," she says. "This looks like... research. Some sort of project."

A newspaper headline catches my eye. "Missing mother," I read. "And here's another. Missing local man."

I open my father's notebook and find a corresponding list. Name, date, and an animal name. I read a few before I realize what the animal means. Grizzly, lion, eagle, raven—they're types of shifters.

"Johnny was looking into missing people," Sunny says and starts stacking the newspaper clippings to one side. In the end there are over thirty, with a few more marked on the list in the notebook.

Not just missing people. Missing shifters.

The foxes were right. Shifters are disappearing. And my father was compiling evidence to prove it.

"What's this?" Sunny lifts a piece of paper, copied from some sort of map. Johnny sketched a few boxes on it, some large, some small, with labels in his neat handwriting.

"Main warehouse, cage area, lab one, lab two," Sunny reads.

"A compound," I say, matching the map to my father's notes. "It's near the Arizona border, just outside the Ute Mountain Reservation. Looks like total wilderness." I get my phone out and look up the coordinates, but Google Earth doesn't show any buildings. "It's a secret facility." I raise my head, and meet my mother's wide eyes. "That's where the missing people end up. See?" I flip to the end of the notebook, where Johnny has dates and notes of trucks moving in and out of the compound. He even noted license plates. "Delivery, October 26th. He found this place and spied on it for over a year." I point to the last date. April 24th of last year. "He thought that something fishy was going on, and the compound was ground zero."

"What does this mean?"

"Johnny didn't just wander off. Neither did these missing people. If his notes are correct, they're not just vanishing into thin air.

"They're being taken."

15

T *ank*

THE BIKE HAS HALF a tank of gas, so I ride a few hours before I take a pit stop. Before I hit the road, I texted Garrett and a few others. Apparently, they had an adventure in Mexico, but everyone's safe home now. They'll debrief everyone at the pack meeting, and I let them know I'd be back in time for that. I'll ride all day without stopping except for gas. Let the road and fresh air shake the memory of the last few days, trippy hippie humans and foxy ladies with *Looney Tunes* hair.

Foxfire. Fuck.

Dad was right. Women are crazy.

I don't even know what happened back there, but I feel like a freight train just ripped through the center of my chest.

When I stop for gas, I turn on my phone. A few missed

calls, the newest from an unknown number, and my dad. I call him back.

"Son?" My dad's voice is strained. Of course, my pack has been through the wringer, and though I've been out of it, he hasn't gotten hold of me.

"Yeah, Dad. It's me. I'm on my way back to Tucson."

"Everything all right?"

"Yeah." I rub my face, feeling about one hundred years old. My wolf is silent, like he's sick. I wonder if my dad felt this way when my mom took off. A loss like missing a limb. "I'm alone."

He hesitates.

"I made a mistake," I tell him. "But it's for the best. I'll be with my pack soon."

"Son." He clears his throat. "I'm sorry things didn't work out. I spoke to your female earlier."

"Yeah?" Foxfire did mention she talked to him.

"I might have been harsher than I needed to be. I was just trying to protect you."

"What did you say? No, it doesn't matter. The mating instinct—you were right. It comes on strong."

"You... was she your mate?"

"Yeah." It's messed up, but there's no denying how my wolf feels for Foxfire. How I feel.

"I didn't know that," my dad mutters.

"What does it matter? Mating instincts mess a wolf up. You always told me that." My bike tank is full. If I hit the road now, I can reach Tucson and not be too late for the meeting. "Anyway, I gotta go—"

"Son, there's something you should know. Your mother—"

"She betrayed the pack. She betrayed you."

"She wasn't my mate."

"What?"

"We were stupid and in love. She wanted me to mark her. But my wolf... he knew. I tried to make it work."

"My mom wasn't your mate?" My head is spinning. "But I thought—"

"I told you, beware the mating instinct. But looking back, I realized I never had it with your mother. The mistake I made—that's on me."

I don't know what to say.

"I did my best to raise you right," my dad goes on. "I did what I could. But you're a man now. You can make your own decisions. And if your wolf decides it's time to take a mate, even if she is a fox..."

"Shifters don't mix. You always told me that."

"I don't know. Times are changing. Your own alpha just took a human mate—"

"What?" My cell phone beeps with a missed message, and I can't handle hearing anything else. "Dad, I've got to go."

"All right, son. Be safe."

The last few days have been crazy, and I'm right back in the twilight zone. My dad just called and told me it's okay to take a mate. I may not have his blessing, but at least he's not going to disown me.

At least not until he sees Foxfire's hairdo and meets her mother.

My cell phone beeps again, impatiently, and I hit the button to listen to my messages.

A soft voice starts talking, and I have to punch up the sound. "Is Jordy. Thought you'd want to know... Foxfire and her mom came by." I tense. "They had a bunch of evidence about the missing shifters and a location—"

A bunch of bikers pull in, their Harleys drowning out

Jordy's near whisper. I stride to the edge of the parking lot to get a little quiet. "The elders refused to help. We're packing up. This place isn't safe for us." A pause. "Don't try to reach me on this number. We'll be gone before Foxfire goes to the compound where the missing shifters might be held. She said you'd left, and I know she's your mate. I just thought you'd want to know."

I listen to the message twice more, then hit redial. Sure enough, the number is disconnected.

Fuck.

I dial Foxfire's number. It goes to voicemail.

"Foxfire. Call me." I text her, too, and call again, chanting, "Pick up, pick up, pick up."

"Hello?" At the sound of her voice, my wolf raises his head.

"Where are you?" I growl.

She doesn't say anything.

"I just got a call from Jordy. She said you found more about missing shifters, including a location where they might be held. So I'll ask again, where are you?"

"What do you care?"

I ignore this. "Don't tell me you're at the compound."

Silence.

"Foxfire." My phone crackles under the strength of my grip. "Your father disappeared. If he was kidnapped, then these people are dangerous."

"I know that. I'm not stupid."

"So what are you going to do?"

Silence.

"Foxfire—"

"I'm going to wait until dark and sneak in." I hear a slight crunch. My cell phone case. I loosen my grip. "What if there are guards?"

"I'm going to set a fire and pull the fire alarm."

"Set a fire?"

"Yeah, just a small one."

"Arson is not a plan." My voice is such a deep growl, it's almost unrecognizable. I will myself to calm down before I shift and go on a rampage. "Baby, just stay where you are. I'll be there soon."

"Don't call me that. I'm not your baby. And I definitely don't want to be your responsibility. I can take care of myself —I always have."

Responsibility? I don't know what the fuck Foxfire is talking about, but we don't have time to discuss it now.

"Give me the address, Foxfire. Don't put yourself in danger. Or your mom. I'm coming for you." I straddle my bike, ready to ride out. "Tell me where you are."

"Go to Tucson. Where you're needed. I don't want you to follow your *compulsion* to take care of me." She hangs up.

I throw my head back and howl. When I'm done, the Harley riders are all staring at me. I snarl at them and pocket my phone. My bike leaves marks on the pavement as I tear off.

A few miles down the road, I start to think clearly. She had time to visit the foxes, and then get to the compound, wherever it is, in the past few hours. If I ever meet those elders again, I'm going to tear them a new one for leaving her unprotected.

You left her first, my wolf reminds me. And he's right. And now Foxfire doesn't even want me to come. Not that I'll let that stop me. I'll never make that mistake again.

I pull off the highway again and make a call. Jackson answers on the first ring.

"Tank?"

I tell him my news in a rush. Jackson is a werewolf and

owns a systems security company worth over a billion. Oh, and his wife's one of the world's best hackers. I already asked him and Kylie to help me track down Foxfire's dad. Explaining doesn't take long.

"What do you need?" Jackson asks. "I have Kylie here."

"Hey, Tank." A bright voice comes on the line. Kylie is young for such a brilliant hacker, a beautiful nerd Jackson mated almost as soon as he laid eyes on her. According to Trey, she's a nerd with a bangin' body. We told Trey never to say that to Jackson's face, unless he wanted an early grave. Jackson may not be our alpha, but he's alpha material, for sure.

"Thanks for all the work you're doing on this," I say quickly, putting as much respect into my tone as I can. "You have no idea what this means to me and my mate."

"No problem." Her warmth comes through the phone. "Glad to help. But there's something you should know. I did a little digging—not too much, Jackson doesn't want the feds after me again."

Jackson mutters something I don't hear.

"I got pretty deep into some... illegal channels. A sort of job board for criminal types."

"Okay," I say, as if I'm following. Which I'm not.

"Foxfire's name was there. Specifically, a low paying job to capture and carry—a kidnapping order."

Chills run up and down my spine.

"There was a bounty for her. A thousand dollars if she was brought in alive."

"What did you say?"

Kylie repeats it, but I'm barely listening. The thug at her door. The mafia men shaking down her mother. It wasn't about Sunny. They were after Foxfire.

"Tank? Are you still there?"

"Yeah. Give me a moment."

There are people snatching shifters. Johnny looked into it, and he was taken. And now they're after Foxfire. Why?

My phone vibrates with a text. I stare at it for a second before I realize what I'm seeing.

"Thought you might need this. —Sunny." Followed by an address. Not a road address, just degrees of longitude and latitude. For better or worse, Foxfire's mother is on my side. Thank fuck for the Queen of La La Land.

"Hang on," I say, "I've got an address." I read Jackson the coordinates.

"There's nothing there," Kylie says after some ferocious typing. "Oh wait. There was something—a building, or a few of them. But it looks like it was updated to show nothing there."

"What does that mean?"

"Something's fishy. Very, very fishy," Kylie says. "I'm on it."

"I'm heading out," I tell them. "I think Foxfire's in danger."

"We'll work on this and be in touch," Jackson promises before they sign off.

I'm itching to get on the road, but there's one more call I need to make. I dial my alpha.

"Hey, Tank, what's—"

"I need backup," I interrupt and rush to fill the shocked silence that follows. Garrett knows I wouldn't interrupt him without good reason. "Foxfire's a fox shifter. Her father was one too, and he's missing. Her kin won't look for him. They say he was snatched by shifters. They've tracked his scent to a warehouse, and Foxfire is about to rush in."

"Shifter snatchers?"

"Foxfire's dad was doing research on them before he

disappeared too, a year ago. Foxfire found out, and now she's going to pick up where he left off." I swallow. Any second now, my alpha's gonna interrupt and order me home. "I know it's sounds crazy, but I think we should help. I'm going to, whatever you decide." Defiance doesn't sit well with wolves. I may be out on my ass.

"Foxfire's a fox," Garrett says slowly.

"Yeah."

"And her dad's been abducted."

"A year ago. He may not be alive." I'm about to tell my alpha I need to go and deal with the consequences later, when Garrett curses.

"We dealt with these fuckers in Mexico. Whatever you do—don't kill them all."

"What?"

"Get your woman to safety. Then call me. Wait—Amber has something to say."

It takes me a second to remember who Amber is. Foxfire's friend. The little human Garrett was sniffing around. My dad said my alpha claimed her as mate.

"Tank," Garrett comes back on the line. "You need to get on the road, now. Amber's psychic, and she says you don't have any time to waste. If you're not there by dusk, Foxfire is in trouble."

16

F oxfire

I RAISE the binoculars and sweep the perimeter of the compound again. I'm up a tree, trying to spy on the compound from the distance. We're on a hill, a little ways away. Not perfect, but the best vantage point I could find without getting close enough to get caught.

"No movement," I mutter. So far, the place has proved pretty boring. There are a few cars in there, but they have been there all day, and other than a few guards who patrol every other hour, I haven't seen any sign of a person.

No vans going in and out today, like my father made note of in his journal. I guess that's something to be glad of. No vans means no deliveries. No kidnapped shifters.

I climb down and make notes in my dad's journal, picking up where he left off. The last entry was so long ago. I try not to imagine what that might mean.

Sunny sits cross-legged in front of Daisy. I expect her to be meditating, but instead she's watching me, brow furrowed.

"I haven't seen anything yet. I'm going to go hike around, see if I can get closer." I need more information if I'm going to break in tonight.

"Do you think that's wise?"

"Do you have a better plan?"

She presses her lips together.

"No," I veto it before I know what she's going to say.

"Honey, really, we need to talk about Tank."

"There's nothing to talk about. He left."

"I can tell you're hurting. He meant something to you."

"We met a few days ago." I can't believe it's only since Saturday. I've lived through several lifetimes. "I barely knew him."

"He's worried about you. He cares about you, too."

If he cared, why did he leave? Oh yeah, because I told him to. Because he doesn't belong with me. "We don't fit, Mom. That's all there is to it."

"All right, dear. I'm sure you know best."

"Yep. I never want to see him again."

Sunny sucks in a breath like she's gonna say something.

"What, Mom?"

"The thing is... I may have told him where we are."

I cuss and check my phone. My signal's not great, so I climb the tree again. Sure enough, I have a bunch of missed calls, some from Amber. Plus a text from Tank.

"Stay where you are. I'm coming. I have a plan to break in tonight. *Do not go in alone.*"

~.~

Tank

At twilight, I reach the compound. I slow my bike and look for a road. Sure enough, there's one cutting through the trees, right where the coordinates indicate the hidden area.

I pass it and circle back, running off the road and hiding my bike in the trees.

I check my phone for a text from Foxfire. Nothing. I told her I have a plan, but that was a bit of a bluff. My plan isn't much better than hers—sneak up to the compound, break in, and snoop around. The only difference is that I'd rather be the one in danger than her.

I dial Jackson and Kylie next.

"Tank?" Kylie answers.

"I'm here," I say quietly. "I'm about a quarter-mile from the compound in the woods."

"Good. Sit tight. Sam is coming to help. He should be arriving at your coordinates now."

I glance around the dark woods. "How do you know my coordinates?"

"I hacked your phone," she says impatiently. "He should be there any minute. He can help you break in and get the data I need."

"What—" I start and whirl at a minute noise several hundred feet to my right. I smell him before I see him.

"He's here," I tell Kylie.

"He'll explain everything. Don't call me again unless you're on a burner phone." She hangs up.

"Sam."

Sam's a young wolf who bartends at Club Eclipse but

isn't a full member of Garrett's pack because he's bound to Jackson, who's a lone wolf.

"Tank." He nods, not quite meeting my eye. I'm more dominant than he is. If I remember the story right, Jackson took him in as a teen runaway. He'd found him on a mountain in wolf form—running wild. He's been that way for months. If Jackson hadn't hunted him down and forced him to shift, Sam would've lost his humanity forever. As it is, he's still a loner. Smart, but keeps to himself, even in a crowd. I'm surprised Kylie would send him. Usually, more dominant wolves are better in combat.

"Kylie says you know the plan?"

He nods. "Garrett and Jackson worked it out."

"Garrett?"

"He called after you did. They came up with everything and sent me."

Sam must've been closer to this place than I was, if he got here so quickly. I don't waste time asking.

"What are we going to do?"

"There's a main building. We're going to wait until 21:00 and sneak in through a hole in the fence. I have bolt cutters. You look around for any captive shifters while I hack their intranet and set up a mole program so Kylie can get into their systems."

"You know how to do that?"

"I live with Jackson King."

"All right." I hold out my hand. "I need your burner phone."

~.~

Foxfire

· · ·

AFTER SUNSET, the temperature drops quickly. I wish I had thought to pick up some food, more than just granola bars.

Something vibrates, and I startle. My phone is off to save the battery from draining in the low service area. My mom holds out hers.

"It's Tank."

I sigh but accept it. The fact that she can even get cell service up here is a minor miracle.

"What do you want?"

"Where are you?"

"My mom already told you that, didn't she? You have a good nose. You figure it out. On second thought," I add hastily, "don't try. I don't want to see you."

"Are you still planning to break in?"

"My dad might be in there. Or, I don't know, he might not be. He might be dead. I'm not naive. I just want answers."

"I'm going to get them for you. In an hour, I'm breaking into the compound."

I clutch the phone. "You are?"

"Yeah, we have a plan. I'm with another shifter, a hacker. He knows how to get into their files. I'm going in and standing guard while he hacks their system. I'll look for your dad."

"If he's there, you'll break him out?"

"Of course."

"Why?"

"Because he's your dad. I called the pack, and told them—"

"You called the pack?" My heart thuds harder.

"Yeah."

I can't believe it. He called the pack for me.

"I need you to take your mom and get away from this place. Foxfire, I mean it. I need you somewhere safe."

"I am safe."

"You're in a VW bus painted bright purple with yellow flowers."

"Actually, it's bright yellow with purple flowers."

"Foxfire—"

"All right, all right. I promise I'll be safe."

"Promise you won't try to storm the compound."

"I won't. I'll stay far away. Just... Tank?"

"Yeah, baby?"

"Be safe. Okay?"

"Baby," he says softly before he hangs up.

17

Tank

It's full dark when Sam and I arrive at the tall chain-link fence topped with barbed wire that surrounds the compound. There are a few small outbuildings, but the two cars in the dirt lot are in front of the large main building.

"That's where the server room is," Sam points out.

"How do you know?"

"Kylie hacked a satellite to get updated images."

I mentally put her on my *don't ever piss off* list and hunch down to wait. There is a hut with a few guards carrying automatic weapons, to keep out anyone entering the road. Most of their security lies in not showing up on any map. Their mistake, our good luck.

I try to get a good scent of the place. It smells like shifters, but not just one type. Wolf, and a few others I'm not familiar with. No fox.

Two men walk out of the building and head to the cars.

Sam brought weapons for us—funny-shaped black guns. "Tranquilizers," he tells me. "Garrett doesn't want any deaths." I rest my hand on it as we wait.

"All right," Sam says when the last car rolls past the guard's gate. We creep around to the back of the compound, and he puts on gloves to use the bolt cutters.

"Wait." I point to a sign that indicates electric current.

"It's off," Sam says. "Not sure why. It was probably built to keep shifters in rather than out."

"Maybe there's no one they need to keep in right now." I hope it's not true. That doesn't bode well for Foxfire's dad.

We crawl through the small hole Sam makes. He pulls it shut behind us so a guard won't notice the breach. From there, it's a short run to the back of the main building. The scent of shifters is much stronger here, clashing with myriad other smells: bleach, chemicals, and cleansing fluid over darker scents. Blood. Fur. Fear.

Under the cover of darkness, we reach a door. I stand watch while Sam crouches to pick the lock. I stop him before he opens it.

"Alarm?"

Sam shakes his head. "They think they're safe."

I hold my breath as he opens it, but nothing triggers. "All right. Go fast. Find the server room."

We follow our noses down a sick-smelling corridor. The harsh cleansers used to clean this place almost numb my nose, but Sam seems to know just where he's going. I follow him, committing a few turns to memory until he comes to a quiet office filled with powered-down machines.

"Here." He pulls a seat up to a computer. "This will be a few minutes."

I hover in the door, keeping watch. The guards should

patrol this place regularly. My hope is that they're complacent. So far, they are. I'd hate to get into a firefight with them. Our weapons will be no match for theirs. Especially if the guards are used to bringing down shifters.

Sam's face is eerily lit by the screen.

"How much longer?" I ask.

"I'm in. Ten minutes."

Just enough time for me to search the building and see if Johnny is here. "Be right back."

I sneak down the hall, following my nose around a few turns. There's a definite animal smell that not even the antiseptic can mask. What sort of shifter, I can't say.

I reach a stairwell and ease the door open. The shifter scent hits me full force, along with the scent of blood and shit. Breathing through my mouth, I descend the stairs. Tingles run up and down my spine as I enter the basement. There are large cages on the other side of the door. The smell is even stronger. This is where they keep their secrets.

Inside, I prowl up and down the rows of empty cages. There are several separate rooms of them, each smelling a little different. Different shifters, I guess. Each room fans off the central one, which is a lab full of racks of test tubes, computers, and tables with heavy restraints. The smell of fear is strongest here. I gag and back out.

One more round of the place, and I reach a wall with small doors leading to cells. I glance in each one, relying on my nose to tell me if anyone's living. There's a few on the end with no window looking in. I almost miss checking when my foot hits the desk nearby and the console comes to life. On screen is a dark room. A camera on one of the cells. As I watch, the shadows move. In the darkness glow two bright eyes.

There's only one creature in here, other than me. A shifter. A prisoner.

I go to the door and rap on it. "Hey. Anyone alive in there?"

I wait a few minutes. Nothing. I need to be getting back up to Sam. I'm about to leave when a growl brings my wolf to high alert.

"Who wants to know?" a deep voice asks.

"I'm a friend. I'm looking for a fox shifter. The father of my mate."

"Are you a prisoner or one of them?"

"Neither. I'm here to get you out." It's the truth. The plan is just to do reconnaissance and wait for the pack to do a full out rescue within the next few nights. "We will free you and whoever else is here, I swear on the life of my mate."

"You here for Johnny?"

"You know him?"

"Get me out, and I'll take you to him."

Damn. That's not the plan. "Is this door alarmed?"

"Not anymore. I'm not the threat I used to be."

Here goes nothing. I study the door. I could try to kick it in, but it's probably built to withstand shifters. "Hang on," I mutter and rip the hinges off, backing up as the door wrenches open from the inside.

"I'm armed," I say as the prisoner climbs out.

"I'm no threat," the shifter growls. He's huge but emaciated, his ribs jutting from his large frame. His scent is rich and smoky.

"What's your animal?"

"You can't smell me, wolf?" He turns his head and gives me the full force of his stare. Golden eyes with a small black pupil. Lion.

I recognize the tattoo on his shoulder.

"Special forces?"

He nods.

"How long have you been here?"

A pause, and then an awful laugh. If I were in wolf form, my fur would stand on end. "Too long. Far too long."

"We don't have much time."

"This way."

I follow him back up the stairs, ears perked for any noises. The hall upstairs is as dark and silent as ever.

"What the fuck were they doing in here?" I mutter as we pass another lab room.

"Experiments on shifters," the tortured lion says. "They're obsessed with bloodline. Sometimes..." His head cocks to the side as if he's remembering something. "Sometimes," he mutters, almost to himself, "they breed them."

I keep my distance as we turn down another hall. I don't have to be a shrink to know this guy is crazy.

"In here," he says. My wolf makes me wait until he backs away to peer through the door.

There's no one in the room. Just a large white box and the smell of ash and death.

"Cremation," my guide rasps. "That's how they get rid of the evidence. You want to find Johnny? He's in there." And he lets out another laugh.

I reel back, gut twisting with the awful sound.

The lion shifter leaps forward and slams my head against the wall. I drop to a knee, dazed. When I find my balance, the lion is gone.

Fuck.

I race back to Sam. He's not at the same computer, but over by the wall. "We got to go."

He rises and hurries to a table to pack up his tools. "What happened to you?"

I swipe at my face. My nose is bleeding.

"Found a prisoner and freed him. We need to move, now."

The prisoner might be smart enough to escape but might not care about not setting off alarms.

Sure enough, as we dart into the hall, lights flood the building. Alarms blare.

"Shit."

"Come on." Sam grabs me and pulls me another way. As we run, shouts hit the building outside.

"What are we going to do? We're surrounded."

"Plan B," Sam says grimly. He pushes me against the wall and presses against it next to me. "Brace yourself."

"Wh—"

A blast shakes the building.

~.~

Foxfire

"Foxfire," my mom calls from her perch atop Daisy. "Something's going on."

"What?" I ask, but as soon as I stand on the seat, hanging out the front door, I can see. There are floodlights on at the compound and alarms blaring. "Oh no."

"What's happening?"

"Trouble," I say. "With a capital T."

~.~

Tank

"WHAT THE FUCK WAS THAT?" I shout as the shock of the blast rings in my ear. The sprinklers cut on, and we run through the slick hall.

"Plan B." Sam doesn't explain.

"You set a bomb?"

"Just in case we needed a diversion." He's creepily calm. Still a slender, mild-looking shifter—apart from the piercings and tats. But there's gleam in his eye I don't like.

"Come on." I race toward the door at the end of the hall. If we're lucky, the guards are distracted enough, we can still escape.

But when I stick my head out, lights flash my way.

"Shit."

"This way. There's another exit."

"How do you know?"

Sam propels me forward. "I've been here before."

I don't have time for the WTF rattling through my brain.

More shouts ring through the building. The guards from the hut are inside, and now it's a game of cat and mouse to make sure they don't find us.

We duck into a room, a normal-looking office.

I crouch behind a desk, muttering curses. Sam squats next to me, an oasis of calm.

"Another ten seconds, and then we run for it." He nods to the window.

I stare at him.

"Wait for it," Sam says, and I brace.

Sure enough, another blast ripples through the building, this one larger, shaking the floor. Sam rushes past me, and I follow, overtaking him to slam feet-first into the glass. It breaks under my flying weight. I roll on the lawn, Sam right behind. We find our feet and pelt toward the fence but don't quite make it before the guards notice us and shout. We slam ourselves to the safe side of a small outbuilding before machine gun fire comes our way.

"Shit," Sam says. "The fence is back on."

Sure enough, the metal hums and crackles with electric charge, probably enough to knock a shifter unconscious.

"There." Sam points to a hole in the fence, metal slashed open.

I give a silent thanks to the newly freed lion. Sure, he was crazy. But I'm beginning to fear Sam could give him a run for his money.

"We can get to it if we have a distraction. Got any more explosives?"

Sam shakes his head.

I hear the guards getting closer and put my hand on my gun. I just hope they're not shooting to kill. Or, if we're captured, that the pack is close behind.

I'm about to dart out and make my last stand when something whistles and pops overhead. Sam and I duck at an explosion. But instead of an earth-shattering blast, the sky lights up with colored lights.

Fireworks. Beautiful, loud fireworks, exploding above the guard tower. A perfect distraction.

"Foxfire," I whisper before grabbing Sam and shoving him first through the shredded hole in the fence toward freedom.

~.~

FOXFIRE

GREEN LIGHTS EXPLODE ABOVE ME.

"That's a little too close for comfort," Sunny calls. I ignore her, lighting three more and letting, them sing off into the night sky. They blossom white, red, and blue. A little early for the Fourth of July. Maybe that's why the guy behind the counter looked at me like I was nuts when I bought out his stock.

"So patriotic!" Sunny crows with delight.

The compound's alive with red alert. Lights, alarms blaring, shots fired.

Hopefully, this is enough of a distraction. We just gotta set them all off and get out of here before someone comes to investigate.

"This one's a big one." Sunny hands me another. I set it up farther away, light the fuse, and run.

A screech, and the sky pops with purple rain.

~.~

Tank

. . .

Sam and I slog up the hill. The alarms and lights are still behind us, along with enough rockets' red glare to make me worried Foxfire won't escape in time. There are guards after us—a few bullets spattered the earth behind us before we took to the woods, but the rest might go after my mate and her mother.

"Where are we going?" I call to Sam and nearly run into a giant blade.

"Here." Sam ducks around me and pulls off the camo netting covering our escape vehicle.

Make that, our escape helicopter.

"Get in." Sam straps himself into the pilot's seat.

"You have a freaking helicopter?"

"It's Jackson's. Kylie found it and thought it'd be cool." He flips switches, and the comms come on. "It's actually a Bell 222, but we modified it for stealth mode." He grins, an eerie sight. "I call it the Air Wolf."

~.~

Foxfire

I shoot the last of our rockets off and run to the car.

"Shut the doors," I scream to Sunny. "We've got to move."

The little bus squeals as I tear out of our hiding place across the road. We pass the compound, still bright and full of chaos. I hope.

"Come on, come on," I whisper to the bus as it chugs up a hill.

"Foxfire, we need to go faster," Sunny reports. "I think they saw us."

Sure enough, a caravan of black Jeeps tears out after us. We pass one coming up the road the opposite way. It does a U-turn and follows.

"Hang on!" I press the gas pedal to the floor. Daisy hurtles down the highway, shaking as it goes faster than it's ever gone before.

It's not enough. The guards are hanging out the Jeep windows, and they have guns.

And they're gaining on us.

~.~

Tank

"Closer," I shout to Sam. We're hovering over the road, our lights spotlighting the action below.

"I can't," Sam says. "They've got guns."

"Closer, goddammit." Foxfire and her mom are in that bus. They're in danger. She risked her life setting off fireworks.

"What are you going to do? Jump on one of the Jeeps?"

"If I have to."

"They're not gonna get anywhere close to her. Just hang on."

"Fuck that." I rise up from my seat, steadying myself as the helicopter dips.

"Nothing's gonna happen," Sam soothes. I'd rip his throat out if he wasn't flying the helicopter. "We got backup."

"What?"

Shots ring out below us. I shout, gripping the side, watching the VW bus from above, helpless.

But Foxfire and her mom don't slow. Instead, the Jeeps skid on the road. Some veer off, others jerk and roll to a stop, blocking the highway. The last vehicles crash into them.

"What's happening?"

"I told you," Sam says. "Backup."

Then I hear it. The roar of motorcycles. One by one, they tear out from under cover where they ambushed the Jeeps. They weave easily around the wreckage. More shots fire, but the bikes all get clear. They zoom down the road and surround the VW bus.

Sam flies overhead, the spotlight skimming a few of the helmets, including two red ones. Jared and Trey got teased mercilessly for choosing that color. They bring up the rear, escorting the VW bus. Leading the pack is a huge Harley. As Sam swoops the helicopter lower, Garrett raises his fist in salute. The rest of the pack does the same, and even though they can't see us, Sam and I raise our fists before zooming back up to cover the pack as they protect my baby and bring her home.

18

T *ank*

I ARRIVE at the roadside motel around midnight. The pack's already here, as well as the little VW bus, hidden behind the place.

Sam lets me down before fleeing in the helicopter to lie low. Good call. I'll bet neither Jackson nor my alpha will be happy with the little bomb stunt he pulled.

The first one to greet me is Garrett. The alpha pulls me into a hug, and we pound each other's backs.

"I oughta beat you," Garrett growls. "I don't care what plan the hackers cook up, next time you wait for your pack."

"I had to go in. Foxfire was going to do it."

Garrett grunts.

"Where is she?"

"Holed up in a room with Amber and her mom. Girl's

night, or something. With all the adrenaline they had going on an hour ago, I bet they've crashed now."

"I was hoping to talk to her." If she'll see me.

"In the morning. We've got news." Garrett leads me to another motel room.

"Hey, man." Jared and Trey greet me with hugs of their own. Human males might not touch each other this much, but shifters do. "Where's Sam?"

"Going to stash the helicopter somewhere. Apparently, it's not quite legal."

"Neither is setting off fireworks in Utah outside of July," Trey says. "I don't even know where you'd buy them."

I keep silent. I wouldn't underestimate Foxfire when it comes to digging up contraband. Or her mother. I picture the two of them flirting with some hapless shop owner, convincing him to sell them, and I want to bash the imaginary guy's teeth in.

"The cops are all over the compound now. I wouldn't be surprised if it's put under investigation."

"Are we in trouble?" There are enough shifters in the government to help with cover-up.

"I think Sam blew up all the evidence. Kylie got most of the data out before then. She and Jackson are going through it now. We'll know more in the morning." Garrett sits on the bed. Trey and Jared toss me a bag of fast food, but I'm too wired to eat, so I grab a drink and down that instead.

"Kylie wants you to know she took down the bounty on Foxfire. She hacked the user account. There were a few older bounties in there, for people all across the US and Canada. We think they were all shifters."

I debrief the room on what I saw in the compound, including a description of the lion shifter. "Someone's snatching shifters and experimenting on them. But why?" I ask.

"We don't know. But we're going to find out," Garrett says. "Jackson called us after I told you Amber's vision. That's when I rallied the pack and asked if Kylie could hack their systems somehow." Garrett explains. "We needed data. We think this operation is connected to the one in Mexico that took my sister."

"What'd you find out in Mexico?" I ask.

"Nothing," Jared cuts in. "We couldn't question anyone because Garrett ate them all."

"They held us captive. And my mate was left unprotected," Garrett says. He doesn't look at all repentant.

"Well, this time we did it right. Or half-right, if we got the data out before the place blew," Trey says.

I shake my head. "Sam is fucking crazy."

Trey and Jared look curious, but I don't elaborate. Sam may have disobeyed orders, but it worked out in the end. I'm not sorry that place is torched. Even if it almost cost me my life. It would've if we hadn't had the fireworks as a distraction.

I rise from where I was leaning against the dresser and start toward the door. I want to see Foxfire. No, I need it.

"Tank," my alpha calls.

Trey and Jared rise, and, with a knowing look at each other, they leave the room.

"Who is Foxfire to you?"

"She's my mate."

"You sure?" He folds his arms across his chest. He's probably protective because Foxfire is his mate's friend, but I still tense.

"I marked her," I half-growl. "She's mine." My wolf has his hackles up.

Garrett studies me, then nods. "Get some sleep. We'll talk more in the morning."

"Where's Foxfire?" My wolf won't rest until he knows she's safe.

Garrett's shoulders soften a little.

"I already told you. Girl's night. They're under guard."

"I'll take a shift."

"No, you'll get some sleep," Garrett says with an alpha's command. "By morning, we should know more about this shifter-snatching black market. I'll need my beta at his best. So will Foxfire."

Despite my alpha's orders, I pace in front of Foxfire's room for a few minutes. I can smell her through the door, beyond the two wolves Garrett posted as guards.

"She's all right." Trey lays a hand on my shoulder.

I'm so wired, I'm about to snap.

"She and Amber debriefed, but there have been no sounds for a while. I think they crashed."

"I should let them sleep," I say, mostly to myself. One part of me knows this, but the other part won't be happy until my mate is in my arms.

If she'll let me hold her.

"It'll be the best for her," Trey agrees, and that decides it. I head to my room and crash.

~.~

Tank

. . .

"I've got good news and bad news," Kylie says through the speaker on Garrett's phone.

"All right, hit us." Garrett leans forward on the bed, propping his elbows on his knees. Jared, Trey, and I stand around the phone, braced for Jackson and Kylie's findings. I checked on Foxfire's hotel room before coming here, but the women are all still asleep. I'm still itching to see Foxfire.

"The good news is, as of this morning, the entire compound is shut down. Human law enforcement is swarming over it because of the bombs and gunfire. They found evidence of prisoner torture, as well the crematorium where the lab destroyed the evidence. No one is getting back in there to do anything any time soon."

"That's good news," Garrett says. "What about the files?"

"Before the feds showed up, the files were completely wiped, including the mole program. They won't find anything to suggest shifters exist."

We all relax. The last thing we need is a branch of the government investigating us.

"Kylie and I spent all night going over the files," Jackson says. "From what we can tell, this was a several year operation, backed by some big money. A shadow corporation. We're going to keep following the trail. But we think it may be tied to the black market shifter operations in Mexico. There was funding from international accounts."

A growl rumbles in Garrett's chest, echoed by Trey and Jared. "Keep us in the know," my alpha says. "The sooner we find these guys, the sooner we can take them out."

"Was there any evidence about the shifters who were kept prisoner?"

A pause. "Unfortunately, yes," Jackson says. "These bastards kept copious notes of their so-called experiments.

They were compiling a DNA database, with every type of shifter represented."

"What about fox shifters?" I ask before anyone else can say anything.

"Just one. A Johnny Red. His chart was linked to Foxfire Hines, with a note to apprehend her." Jackson clears his throat, and I realize my wolf is growling.

"I'm sorry." Kylie comes on the line, her voice full of sympathy. "His file was labeled *deceased*."

Damn. I need to break the news to Foxfire.

"From what I've read, they wanted Foxfire because she was the daughter of a shifter and a human. The whole operation is centered around breeding new shifters that aren't *defective*, whatever that means."

"It means they can still shift," Garrett explains. "Shifter rates have been decreasing because birth rates are down. Some packs ban human-shifter relationships because they believe bloodlines get watered down. More children are born without an animal."

"So when they found out Johnny had a daughter, they wanted to bring her in," I say. "But the only link they had was Sunny. So they went to her first."

"Kylie already deleted the bounty on Foxfire, but she might still be in danger. Along with her mother," Jackson adds.

"We'll send someone from Dad's pack to get Sunny's trailer. We're moving it to pack land until we're sure she's safe," Garrett assures me.

Noise from outside interrupts. The wolf guard outside the door is barring someone entry to our room.

"Well, I'm his mate." Amber's voice rises.

Garrett's on his feet in a flash, heading to the door. "Let her in," he orders.

A moment later, the human female storms in. "Where is he?" She pushes past my alpha and comes to stand in front of me. "What the hell is wrong with you?"

"Excuse me?"

"You hurt Foxfire!" she cries, getting right in my face. "She was on the rebound. She didn't need you to play games with her heart while she's dealing with her family crises."

I surge to my feet. "What the fuck?" *What's wrong with Foxfire?*

I *knew* I needed to see her last night.

"What's going on, Amber?" Garrett growls, coming up to stand protectively beside her.

"He marked her without asking and then totally left!"

"She's my mate," I snap. "And I wasn't leaving—" Fuck this. I needed to explain to Foxfire, not these boneheads. "Where is she?"

"She's leaving," Amber snaps.

"What?"

"Something you said to her. You marked her and then refused to claim her because shifters don't mix. She thinks you don't want her."

I reel back as if struck.

Amber doesn't seem to notice. "She says she's moving." Amber grips Garrett, appealing to him with wide blue eyes. "She's all worked up about not inconveniencing the pack, whatever that means."

"Where is she?" I'm halfway to the door.

"Gone. Headed back to Tucson. I tried to stop her, but—"

I rush out. Sure enough, the back parking lot is empty of the VW bus.

"Tank?" Trey's at my side. I push him away.

"I've got to go."

"Tank—" Garrett's in the doorway, Amber by his side.

"I claim Foxfire Hines as my mate," I thunder so everyone can hear. I'll get a bullhorn if I have to. Or pay Sam to fly a banner around the world.

"What are you going to do?" Amber asks. She doesn't look mad anymore. She looks relieved. Women. Crazy.

"Make sure she knows she's mine." I turn to Garrett. "Do I have your blessing?"

Garrett's lips twitch. "Do you need it?"

"No," I tell him. "Foxfire's mine, whether I'm welcome in the pack after this or not."

My alpha pulls his mate closer. "Foxfire is welcome in our pack. Go get your mate."

"Here." Trey tosses me his keys.

The rest of the pack breaks into whoops as I run to the bike.

19

F *oxfire*

"ARE YOU SURE, HONEY?" Sunny stands in my doorway, brow furrowed, a cup of green tea in her hand. The whole way home, she bit her lip and gave me worried looks.

As soon as I got to my little house in Tucson, I started packing. My stomach is in knots, and I'm having a hard time not crying, but I have to get the hell out of here.

"Totally sure. I can work from anywhere." I pull my underwear drawer out and dump it into my suitcase.

"I just think you should talk to him."

Been there, done that, got the rejection. I don't fit in Tank's world. And I care enough about him to not ruin his place in the pack. So, yeah, this may feel like I've gouged my own heart out and tossed it in the garbage can, but it's what I have to do.

A roar of motorcycle pipes makes my head snap up. Oh god, no. If I see him, I won't be able to be strong.

"I'll just go see who it is." Sunny hurries out.

I know who it is, even before I catch his scent.

I'd run, but he can chase me. And my fox doesn't want to leave him. She's drunk on Tank juice. High on wolfie love. Whatever.

The big wolf unfolds from the Harley and strides up my drive like he owns the place. I watch from the window, my arms folded my arms across my chest. I'm not going down so easily.

"Tank, so nice of you to visit," my mother trills.

"Sunny," he says. "Where's Foxfire?"

"In her room. She's packing," my mom adds in a whisper.

Heavy boots start my way. When Tank comes into view, he takes my breath away. He's so big, he fills the whole door. I forgot how hot he is.

"Foxfire."

"Tank." I hold my ground, but I want to run to him and climb him like a tree.

"We need to talk."

"Listen, let's not make this hard. I know I'm not right for—"

"Honey?" Sunny calls from the other room. "One of Tank's friends just pulled up with my trailer. I'm just going to go with him, okay?"

"Okay, Mom," I call.

Before the front door closes, Tank is moving.

"I know we don't fit together—" I can't finish my sentence because he's kissing me. He hoists me in his arms, and my legs twine around his waist. His lips latch onto mine, plundering, devouring. Needy noises escape my throat. I pull his shirt up as he walks me backward to the bed.

"Wait, wait," I say as he lays me down. "I'm still mad at you." More like hurt, and desperately needy, and not wanting to feel this way ever again because the pain is killing me.

"I know." He kneels next to the bed. He peels my jeans off and fastens his mouth to my foxy bits. Apparently, I'm incapable of protesting.

My legs kick and then clamp around his head as he stabs me with his tongue. My hips rise off the bed.

"Wh-what are you doing?"

"Showing you who you belong to, baby."

I buck against his mouth, grab his ears, and pull him tighter. "You—you can't just stomp in here and start kissing my foxy bits and—" I scream as I come.

Tank arches an eyebrow. "You were saying?"

I shake my head. "Tank, this isn't for the best."

He rises over me, shedding his shirt. "Baby, you're wrong. You and me, we belong together, and I don't care if I have to turn my back on everyone else in my life to keep you. You're mine. I marked you. I'm your man now."

My resolve is nonexistent. I reach for him. Ten seconds later, his jeans are off and I have him. My legs grip him as he thrusts. My bed rocks as he slams into me. And not just the bed. My whole world.

The wall goes *thump, thump, thump* as he flips me over and finishes. His teeth scrape my shoulder, my neck. I shudder.

He turns me to face him. "I'm sorry I left."

"I pushed you away."

"Never again." His face is so serious, I know it's a vow.

I touch his jaw.

He captures my hand and kisses my palm.

"Tank," I whisper.

"Baby, are you shaking?"

I am. I roll to my side, facing the wall. "If you leave again, it'll destroy me. I thought I was strong, but I'm not."

"Baby. You are strong. But you don't have to fight anymore. That's why I'm here. I was born to protect you."

"I'm not changing who I am." My voice quivers.

"I don't want you to."

"But how will we—"

"We'll make it work, baby. We were meant to be together." He pulls me back to face him and grips the back of my neck. "Foxfire, I'm claiming you."

I cling to him.

"Baby." His lips move against my forehead, down to my temple.

"Are you sure?"

He tips my face up to his. "I live my life in black and white. And you." He sifts a hand through my hair, spreading the rainbow strands out on pillow. "You're color."

"Is that a bad thing?"

He rolls so I'm nestled underneath him. His arms hold his giant body so his weight doesn't crush me.

"It's a good thing, baby. A very good thing."

He kisses me, only breaking it off when there's a sound of wood splintering. The mattress under us sags.

"Tank?"

"Mmm?"

"I think we broke the bed again."

~.~

Foxfire

THAT NIGHT, the moon rises huge and golden. Tank wraps me in a blanket and takes me outside. We have a picnic on the deck, and when it gets too cold, I end up in his lap.

"You ready to meet the pack?" he asks.

"Maybe. I don't know. I'm scared."

"You're not scared of anything."

"Except toilet snakes."

"I'll be there. I'm gonna protect you."

"Yeah?" I turn and wrap the blanket around him.

"Always." He lifts me and carries me back inside.

"I love you," I tell him as he sets me down.

"I know, baby."

"Wait, you're not going to say it back?"

"I love you." He punctuates his words with kisses. "I love everything about you."

"Even though I'm crazy?"

"The way you drive me crazy, I don't wanna be sane." Another kiss, and he raises his head. "What did I say about calling yourself names?"

"Punishment?" I say hopefully.

He sits up on the edge of the bed and crooks his finger at me.

EPILOGUE

One week later...

Foxfire

"Do you have it?" I bounce up and down as Tank produces a new helmet. It's red and yellow and orange like a sunset. Like my new hairdo.

I pull the helmet on and scamper to his motorcycle.

"Arms around me at all times. No funny business." More rules.

"Yeah, yeah, got it."

"You misbehave," he threatens, "you get punished."

Yum.

"Got it, big man. Can we go now?"

Tank sighs.

Despite his misgivings, the ride goes off without a hitch. We reach our destination right at dusk: Tucson billionaire Jackson King's mansion, which abuts the Catalina mountains, where the pack will be running tonight.

The scent of wolves hits me as I swing off Tank's bike. He takes my hand and leads me forward, stopping when I hang back.

"Are you sure they're going to like me?" I smooth down my hair.

"Of course, baby." Tank gives me a hug. "And if they don't, I'll kick their asses."

I giggle. He would, too. Amber told me no one protested when Garrett announced I was joining the pack as Tank's mate. If there was any rebellion about a fox shifter joining the ranks, it was quickly quelled by my new alpha or his second.

We walk up the drive to the mansion. "I can't believe you didn't tell me Jackson King was a wolf," I whisper to Tank.

"Yep. And his mate and her grandmother are panthers."

The door opens before we approach, and Jared sticks his head out.

"Finally. The fox is here!"

Kylie, Jackson's mate, greets me and introduces me to Jacqueline, her grandmother.

Wild whoops greet us as we walk through the foyer to the large living area. The pack is all here, most holding red Solo cups or bottles of beer.

"Hiya, foxy," Trey called from the corner. Tank growls, but I give him a little wave.

"Haven't seen you around much lately." Jared hands me a red Solo cup filled with something.

"Tank's been keeping me home a lot," I say. It's true, Tank decided the best way to punish me for leaving him was to place me under house arrest for a whole week and fuck me until I couldn't walk. The bed frame collapsed after a few hours.

"Hear that, boys?! Ole Tank is house trained."

"If my lady was half as foxy, I wouldn't leave the house either," another wolf mutters.

"That's enough," Tank growls.

"Thanks, guys." I smile and wave. Trey starts doing introductions but only gets half through them before Tank hauls me into a bedroom.

"What did I tell you about flirting?"

"I wasn't flirting. Sheesh. I was just being friendly."

Tank pulls down the neck of my shirt, nuzzling the mark he left. He kisses and licks it, and I know I'll have a bright red hickey on top of my mark for the rest of the night. Which is exactly his plan.

I go weak-kneed until he starts to herd me to the bed.

"Tank, not here! We'll break it!"

He growls again but tugs my shirt back into place and leads me out. Everyone in the living room cheers. I blush, grateful when Tank pulls me outside to where Garrett is manning two huge grills. Amber turns from a picnic table stacked with platters of meat.

"Foxfire," she squeals, and we greet each other. "I didn't know you were here! Garrett was showing me the pool room. I must have been... distracted." Her hair is mussed, and her neck sports a hickey of its own.

"The guys gave me a warm welcome."

"Ignore them." Amber rolls her eyes. "They're like a bunch of frat boys who happen to get hairy under the full moon. Hey, did you have a chance to talk to your mom yet?"

"No. I need to. I've been... busy all week."

"You should talk to her. She's all settled in at the clubhouse... and apparently she knew more about shifters than she was letting on."

"What?" I gasp. "She knows?"

"She knew everything," Garrett says. "She asked me flat out if a wolf was my spirit animal."

"I've never seen Garrett look so shocked." Amber giggles. "Sunny said she saw with her third eye."

"Makes sense," I muse. "She did name me Foxfire. On some level, she always knew."

"What does this mean?" Tank asks.

"I sat her down and told her everything. Swore her to secrecy. I've been having a wolf watch over her for the past week. Someone from my dad's pack, actually." Garrett winks at Amber, and she smiles knowingly.

"Yeah?" Tank looks suspicious. "Who?"

The roar of a motorcycle interrupts. We all turn as two riders, one male, one female, swing off the bike.

"Mom?" I gasp. Tank and I head to the driveway to greet her, slowing as we get closer. Sunny's wearing a leather jacket over her peasant blouse and skirt. A big guy with steely gray hair helps her out of it. He looks vaguely familiar.

"Dad?" Tank looks stunned.

"Son." The big man—wolf shifter by the smell of him— greets Tank. He nods at me. "Foxfire. A pleasure. I've heard so much about you."

"Is this who you've been staying with?" I ask Sunny.

"Yes, darling." She comes and leans into Tank's dad. He puts an arm around her.

"Is your alpha here?" Titus asks his son. "My alpha has a message for him."

"Over there, sir."

"Later, darling." My mom waves as Titus leads her away.

I put a hand on Tank's chest to steady myself. "Are our parents...?"

"I don't want to talk about it."

"Agreed. Let's never talk about it again." I am not thinking about my mom having sex. I am not thinking about my mom having sex. I am not... dammit.

I take a big gulp of the contents of my Solo cup and offer it to Tank, who tosses back the rest. "Let's get more booze."

"Agreed."

The rest of the night is fun. I learn that Tank's real name is Titus, Jr. His dad and my mom met when Garrett needed someone to tow Tank's truck and Mom's trailer back from Flagstaff.

After dinner, where I stuff myself with more meat than I've eaten in my entire life, Sunny pulls me aside.

"Everything okay?" I ask as she closes the bedroom door for some privacy. I really, really hope she's not going to talk about her relationship with Tank's dad. Or ask me about sex positions and demo them, nude. You never know with Sunny.

"I need to show you something." She pulls a little package from her purse. "These came to the clubhouse yesterday. Same PO box as the one your dad used. They were addressed to the club, but inside there was a note for you."

I pull open the package.

Foxfire, reads the note. *These were in Johnny's things. Thought you might want them.*

It's not signed, but I can guess who sent it. I only hope Jordy and the rest of the foxes are safe. Maybe one day she'll be able to visit me. I'd love to dye her hair and buy her some new clothes.

The note is wrapped around some old pictures. I spread them out and suck in a breath. They're all of me.

"Every time I got an envelope of money, I sent him one," Sunny says as I lift them one at a time. There's a Polaroid of me in my pink tutu when I was four.

"You wore that for a year. I couldn't get you to take it off."

Another one of me winning the science fair with my display of the strata of the Grand Canyon. More of me at school, including a prom picture.

"That was the first time you dyed your hair. Turquoise to match your dress."

"More like puke green." I shake my head. The color makes me look ill. "I can't believe you sent all these and he kept them."

"Oh, darling." Sunny hugs me, and I realize my cheeks are wet. Voices murmur outside, and the door opens.

"Baby." Tank folds me in his arms. His hand soothes up and down my back as I cry it out, like I did when Tank broke the news of my father's death.

"He loved me." My voice is muffled in his shoulder. "He really did."

"Of course he did. What's not to love?"

That makes me cry more.

Amber comes in with tissues, and after a bathroom session with emergency makeup, I'm able to join the party once more. No one comments on my red eyes, although Trey sneaks a hug—finishing quickly when Tank growls at him. Jared gives me a fist bump, and Amber beckons me to the edge of the deck to stand with her and Garrett.

"We have a surprise for you," my new alpha tells me. "Just our little way of welcoming you into the pack."

The pack all gathers on the deck, looking up at the sky and growing quiet.

"Was this your idea?" I ask Tank.

"Nope."

"It was the pack's," Trey offers. "But Tank's dad bought everything."

"His way of apologizing," Tank mutters.

I search the crowd but don't see Titus.

"He's over there." Garrett points to the bushes a distance from the house.

A whistle, a pop, and white sparks light up the sky.

"Fireworks," I breathe.

"For my baby." Tank's hands steady my hips as fireworks bloom red, yellow, green, blue, and purple over and over again.

"Rainbow colors," Trey points out and tugs a lock of his hair.

A light show, just for me.

Tank takes my hand. "It's time."

He pulls me to the side. Amber and Sunny wave to me as they head inside. The rest of the pack is already stripping off their clothes.

Garrett changes first, points his nose to the moon, and bays. He glances back in Amber's direction and waits for her wave before dashing off into the brush.

The rest of the pack follows, the change spurred by their alpha's call.

Tank stands guard as I step into the poolhouse to change.

"Are you sure?" I ask. "You don't want to just run with the pack?"

"Baby." He shakes his head. "You are pack."

A minute later, I trot out in fox form. Tank sniffs me over and escorts me carefully to the hill where Garrett waits. The big alpha approaches, and I roll to my back, offering my belly in trust and submission. A cursory sniff, and Garrett steps away. Tank takes his place until I'm on my feet again. He takes the rear, Trey and Jared flank me, and Garrett leads the way. We run as another round of fireworks explode in the night sky.

THANK you for reading *Alpha's Challenge*! We would appreciate your review. Be sure to grab the next book in the series, *Alpha's Obsession.*

WANT MORE? ALPHA'S OBSESSION

Please enjoy this excerpt from Alpha's Obsession, the next book in the series.

Layne

THE COMPUTER DATA stares at me and I stare back. It's a pointless contest. The computer wins.

Shaking my head, I roll my chair across the lab to my microscope, but no, nothing's changed there either. "That can't be right," I mutter and rub my eyes. I've been peering through the microscope or at a screen all day, seven days a week since starting this job. Maybe I'm starting to hallucinate.

"Something wrong?"

I gasp and whirl, hand to my chest. "Dr. Smyth, you startled me."

The man at the door inclines his white blond head but doesn't apologize.

"Nothing's wrong. Just talking to myself. I do that sometimes. Um." I clear my throat. "I finished with the preliminary tests with the cells the Alpha team rushed over. There have been some rather spectacular results."

My boss walks in like he owns the place, even though he hasn't set foot in here since he first hired me. He isn't dressed in a lab coat, but in a dark business suit. Even in shiny black shoes, he doesn't make a noise when he moves, and sometimes I catch him watching me with an unblinking stare. Like an alligator or some predator on the hunt. My mother always told me I had a wild imagination. I clutch my desk chair, happy to have something between me and him.

"I have to ask—what was the source of these cells?"

"I'd tell you, but then I'd have to kill you." His smile makes me stiffen. If anything, the mirthless grimace only showcases his prominent canines.

"Ah yes, of course." I give a half-hearted laugh, to show I know it was a joke.

"All in due time, Miss Layne. For now, Data-X is enforcing double blind tests on all new projects, to prevent research bias in the findings."

"Of course. It's just, the data... it's extraordinary." I move to my desk to show him. "Everything was normal until I placed them under a high spectrum—"

"One moment," My boss interrupts and waves in someone from the hall. A lean, older man with a seamed face walks in. "Don Santiago, I'd like you to meet our new hire, the leading scientist on the Omega project. Miss Layne Zhao."

Actually, it's Doctor Zhao. I worked hard for that Ph.D.

Someday I'm going to have the nerve to correct this creep with a crocodile smile.

The newcomer's eyes crawl up and down my form. He's either judging my rumpled appearance, or admiring my breasts under my lab coat. I decide it's the former, to give him the benefit of a doubt.

"Nice to meet you." I straighten, wishing I'd known my boss was coming with guests. I can't remember the last time I went home to shower. Not that I'd have much time, but at least I could've put on a fresh lab coat and brushed my hair. I can't remember the last time I did any of those things, either. Which isn't keeping Don Creepy from eye-fucking me.

"The pleasure is mine," the man purrs in heavily accented English. His gaze rests on the curve of my breasts under the lab coat as he says to Smyth, "Such a beautiful woman to keep locked up in this lab."

Smyth chuckles and I grip the chair. Something about the grating sound puts my teeth on edge.

"Oh, we'll let her out eventually." To me he says, "Don Santiago is visiting all our operations. He's a major donor to the program. I'd like him to hear your findings."

"Of course." I pause as several black clad men stride in and take places by the door and discreet places around the room. They all carry automatic weapons strapped to their chest.

"My apologies," Santiago says in that warm, rich tone. "I bring my bodyguards wherever I go. Things are less secure in my home country."

"Ah, right. No problem. Security around here is pretty tight, too." I smile weakly. Truth is, security around here is ridiculous. Another reason I work such long hours in the lab—so I don't have to go through the stupid strip search every time I take a break or leave for lunch. Some of the security guards enjoy searching me a little too much.

"A necessary precaution," Smyth says. "Our research is on the cutting edge of DNA studies. Our competition would kill to get their hands on our findings." I stiffen again at the word kill, but both Smyth and Santiago chuckle. Being surrounded by six burly guards with guns must put me on edge.

I clear my throat. "As I was saying, these are the cells extracted from the Alpha project—you're familiar with it?"

Both Smyth and Santiago nod. They probably know more about it than I do.

"So I'm running tests on these cells. And... they're extraordinary. Resistant to disease, extremely long lasting and self-regenerating." I pause for gasps of awe.

Nothing. The two men watch me. Santiago almost looks... bored. Smyth gestures for me to continue.

"But they're normal human cells... at least I thought they were." I turn to the computer where I ran the latest test. "Today I placed them under a weak light spectrum. The cells... morphed. Into something else. Something... not human. I haven't been able to discover much beyond that—"

"What sort of light spectrum initiated the changes?"

"Uh." I hate when I'm interrupted, and Smyth does it a lot. But he's the boss, and when he hired me, he gave me access to a state of the art facility to complete my post-doc studies. And when I publish my findings, all the creep factors here will be worth it. That's what I keep telling myself, anyway. Just smile and comply. "It's uh..." I search for layman's terms. "Made mostly of red and orange. A weak light. Meant to simulate moonlight."

Smyth and Santiago exchange glances.

"Anything else?" Santiago asks. I shake my head, even though I want to gush on about how amazing the breakthrough is.

"Good, good. Email me with any more findings." Smyth holds out a hand to usher Santiago from the room, immediately dismissing me.

I bite my tongue. I'm a DNA scientist. I have degrees from two top schools. And now I have a boss who treats me like an idiot lab tech, or worse, eye candy. And I'll take it, because if these Alpha cells hold the key to curing disease, then being a little uncomfortable is worth it.

I sigh and get back to work.

~.~

A FEW HOURS LATER, the lights flicker above me, and I blink. For a second the lab is bathed in darkness, the only light coming from the computers. I stand, but they come back on, as if everything's normal. My computers are all running, but they're on backup generators so if there's a power outage, I don't lose any data. Still, it's odd.

"Security," a low voice calls and I rear up from the desk. A young man with spiky blond hair holds up his hands. He's wearing black jeans and a black t-shirt molded to his muscled chest. He's not a big guy, like some of the security guards, but he is pure lean muscle. Something about him makes my near-extinct libido rev its engine.

"Hey, sorry. Didn't mean to scare you."

"It's all right. Um, do you need me to go?" I gather up some papers.

"No, I won't be here long. Are you on the night shift?"

I flash him a smile. He's young for a security guard—my age. Tattoos run up his forearms and he has gauges in both ears. Even so, he's friendly-looking, and not in a creepy way.

"I'm just working late. Ongoing project. You know how it is."

"I'll be quick," he says. "Just doing the rounds."

"Got it. They sure don't skimp on the security around here."

Another low laugh. He's a little James Dean. Or Billy Idol. Not like the other military-type guards. "I promise not to get in your way." His voice is smoky.

"Thank you." This earns him a bigger smile. My lab is my kingdom and sanctuary. As much time as I spend here, it should be my permanent address.

I pinch the bridge of my nose to relieve the ache between my eyes. It's nighttime, which means dinner. I haven't even eaten lunch.

I head to the corner where I keep my granola bars and pain meds, feeling the young guard's eyes on me. He's attractive, if you pay attention to things like that. Which I usually don't. For whatever reason, my hormones, which have barely worked since I skipped high school and went straight to college, just kicked into gear. Over the first friendly security guard in this prison-like work environment. Go figure. I definitely need to get out more.

I use the break to go to the bathroom, where I splash water on my face. Other than dark circles under my eyes, I don't look too horrible. My straight black hair is pulled into a tight ponytail, no muss, no fuss. I have high cheekbones and dimples, like my mother, with almond-shaped eyes, a gift from my Chinese-American father. I guess I'm pretty. Even in a lab coat, my curves are obvious. Not as full as they would be if I ate regularly. But under the white fabric is a woman's body. Enough to entice skeevy security guards. Enough to draw Santiago's attention.

I make a face at the mirror. I don't care if he's a donor and multi-millionaire—and he must be, to fund a project like this. That dude was creepy. I don't want him ogling me. The young security guard... now that's a different matter. Wouldn't mind a strip search from him.

Okay, that was an uncharacteristically sexual thought. What's going on with me? I really have been too isolated lately.

When I return to my seat, the computer flickers. Odd. It was fine a minute ago. But now the screen is alive with movement.

What the hell? I frown, my fingers flying for the mouse. My research is on this computer and I don't have time for IT problems.

I look over and see the young security guard bent at a modem in the corner. "What are you doing?"

He straightens, but doesn't answer.

"The only person who's supposed to touch these computers is me."

He shoves his hands in his pockets and for some reason, I think he's doing it to seem less threatening.

"Did Dr. Smyth send you?"

The handsome guard goes still. Fully alert. "You know Dr. Smyth?"

"Of course I do. He hired me. He was just here."

"Here?" The man's mouth tightens, blue eyes blaze. "Did you see him?"

"Yes. Why?" The computer beeping beside me makes me turn. "What did you do?" Numbers scroll across the screen, some sort of code I don't recognize. "These machines are used only for tabulating my test results." I hit the keyboard and nothing happens. "Did you do this? Make it stop!"

When I turn, he's pointing a gun at me. A large handgun with an extra barrel on top. "Step away from the computer," he says. "I don't want to hurt you."

My heart jams up in my throat. I raise my hands and back away. Gone is the casual, harmless air, replaced by a hard-faced soldier.

Who in the hell is this guy and what does he want? Suddenly the security in this building doesn't seem so over the top. Maybe they really do have people who want to steal the research. If I can get into the hall, I can pull an alarm. My eyes must've flashed in that direction because he shakes his head.

"Don't even think about it."

My blood runs hot, then cold. "What are you going to do?"

"What I have to. No more, no less. Do as I say and you have nothing to worry about." Says the man holding the gun. I keep still, mentally tallying everything in this place I could use as a weapon. There are a few vials of infectious diseases in a cold room, but if I throw them at him, I'm putting myself at risk. Keeping the gun trained on me, the intruder moves to the computer and waits.

"A few more minutes, and I'll be on my way. This lab is rigged with explosives, though. So you'll want to get out quick."

Ice sluices through my veins. "What? No," I gasp. "You're bluffing."

"I don't bluff."

I grip the back of a chair to keep upright, the tidal wave in my stomach making me dizzy. "Why are you doing this?

This research could save lives." My brain spins, working on how to get my data out of the place before it blows.

"Is that what they told you to get you to work here?" He has an eerie calm about him. A quiet intelligence that keeps me from writing him off as a lunatic.

How could I have mistaken him for a security guard? When he turns his eyes on me, I see I was wrong—they aren't blue. They glow a weird yellow color. Or maybe it's a trick of the light.

"They lied."

"No, it's the truth. I should know. I've been working on this project half my life. And I'm so close to a break-through." I can't stop myself from turning to the printer and grabbing the reams of paper printout. "Please, my findings will mean so much to people. People with no hope—" my breath catches on a sob. I don't usually wear my heart on my sleeve. Guess having my life threatened brings it out.

He takes a soft step forward and studies my face a moment. "What did you find?"

"The cells I'm working on—they're resistant to disease. Not only that, they regenerate. I'm almost done extracting their DNA sequence. Once I do that, I'll be able to replicate it."

Something flickers in his expression, but I can't quite read it. "And then what?"

"Then... I'll use it to help people. People who are sick. People who have debilitating, life-threatening diseases, and no other options. This can help so many." I stop as the lights flicker again.

They come back on, pause, as if holding their breath. Then cut off for good and we're plunged into darkness. I can only see by the green gleam of the exit sign over the door. The young guard hasn't moved, and I realize—this is part of his plan. His handsome face is almost weary in the low light of the computer screens.

"I'm sorry," he says.

Something in me snaps. I run toward the door. He's on me in a flash, arms banding around me from behind. I open my mouth to scream and he clamps a hand over my mouth. It occurs to me he didn't use the gun. Why not?

"Calm down." He carries me backwards. I'm smaller than him, and he's also freakishly strong. "I don't want to hurt you. I just want to know more about Dr. Smyth. Where is he now? In the facility?" He smells like pine trees and warm earth. Maybe it's a sign that I've been cooped up alone here too long, but his arms feel nice around me—as if he's giving me a hug, not restraining me. And I'm not as freaked out as I probably should be. Still, I can't have him ruining my research. He slowly peels his fingers from over my mouth.

"I don't know anything. Please. I was just hired a few months ago!"

"But you saw him today?"

I nod.

"Was he with anyone?"

"An old man—a donor. Don Santiago. He had lots of bodyguards," I add. "Like ten of them. Men with guns. Militia." I don't know if I tell him that part to scare him or because I need to share it with someone because I found it so bizarre.

The young man turns me so I face him. He holds both my forearms in a firm but not bruising grip. Something about his closeness brings my body to life, my nipples tingly and hot, heat pooling between my legs. But it's insane to be attracted to a criminal.

"Are they *in the building*?"

I shake my head. "No, I think they left."

"Where did they go? Does Smyth have an office here?"

"Please..."

"Answer me!" he snaps.

"No! I don't know where he works. We usually conference by phone or video." I peer up at him in the darkness. His eyes are ancient in his youthful face. He's lived a hard life, whoever he is.

"What's your name?"

"Dr. Zhao. Layne." I add my first name, hoping he'll see me as a person, not some faceless lab rat. I lick my lips. Briefly, his gaze falls to them. Indecision plays over his face.

"All right, Layne." He rotates me to pin both my wrists behind my back. "You're coming with me."

READ MORE

READ ALL THE BAD BOY ALPHA BOOKS

Bad Boy Alphas Series
Alpha's Temptation
Alpha's Danger
Alpha's Prize
Alpha's Challenge
Alpha's Obsession
Alpha's Desire
Alpha's War
Alpha's Mission
Alpha's Bane
Alpha's Secret
Alpha's Prey
Alpha's Blood
Alpha's Sun

Shifter Ops
Alpha's Moon
Alpha's Vow
Alpha's Revenge

Midnight Doms
Alpha's Blood
His Captive Mortal
Additional books by other authors

WANT FREE BOOKS?

Go to reneeroseromance.com to sign up for Renee Rose's newsletter and receive a free copy of *Theirs to Protect, Owned by the Marine, Theirs to Punish, The Alpha's Punishment, Disobedience at the Dressmaker's* and *Her Billionaire Boss*. In addition to the free stories, you will also get special pricing, exclusive previews and news of new releases.

Go to www.leesavino.com to sign up for Lee Savino's awesomesauce mailing list and get a FREE Berserker book —too hot to publish anywhere else!

OTHER TITLES BY RENEE ROSE

Paranormal

Bad Boy Alphas Series

Alpha's Temptation

Alpha's Danger

Alpha's Prize

Alpha's Challenge

Alpha's Obsession

Alpha's Desire

Alpha's War

Alpha's Mission

Alpha's Bane

Alpha's Secret

Alpha's Prey

Alpha's Sun

Shifter Ops

Alpha's Moon

Alpha's Vow

Alpha's Revenge

Wolf Ranch Series

Rough

Wild

Feral

Savage

Fierce

Ruthless

Untamed

Wolf Ridge High Series

Alpha Bully

Alpha Knight

Midnight Doms

Alpha's Blood

His Captive Mortal

Alpha Doms Series

The Alpha's Hunger

The Alpha's Promise

The Alpha's Punishment

Other Paranormal

The Winter Storm: An Ever After Chronicle

Contemporary

Chicago Bratva

"Prelude" in Black Light: Roulette War

The Director

The Fixer

"Owned" in Black Light: Roulette Rematch

The Enforcer

Vegas Underground Mafia Romance

King of Diamonds

Mafia Daddy

Jack of Spades

Ace of Hearts

Joker's Wild

His Queen of Clubs

Dead Man's Hand

Wild Card

Daddy Rules Series

Fire Daddy

Hollywood Daddy

Stepbrother Daddy

Master Me Series

Her Royal Master

Her Russian Master

Her Marine Master

Yes, Doctor

Double Doms Series

Theirs to Punish

Theirs to Protect

Holiday Feel-Good

Scoring with Santa

Saved

Other Contemporary

Stolen by the Zandian

Other Sci-Fi

The Hand of Vengeance

Her Alien Masters

Regency

The Darlington Incident

Humbled

The Reddington Scandal

The Westerfield Affair

Pleasing the Colonel

Western

His Little Lapis

The Devil of Whiskey Row

The Outlaw's Bride

Medieval

Mercenary

Medieval Discipline

Lords and Ladies

The Knight's Prisoner

Betrothed

The Knight's Seduction

The Conquered Brides (5 book box set)

Held for Ransom (out of print)

Renaissance

Renaissance Discipline

ALSO BY LEE SAVINO

Paranormal romance

The Berserker Saga and Berserker Brides (menage werewolves)

These fierce warriors will stop at nothing to claim their mates.

Draekons (Dragons in Exile) with Lili Zander (menage alien dragons)

Crashed spaceship. Prison planet. Two big, hulking, bronzed aliens who turn into dragons. The best part? The dragons insist I'm their mate.

Bad Boy Alphas with Renee Rose (bad boy werewolves)

Never ever date a werewolf.

Tsenturion Masters with Golden Angel

Who knew my e-reader was a portal to another galaxy? Now I'm stuck with a fierce alien commander who wants to claim me as his own.

Contemporary Romance

Royal Bad Boy

I'm not falling in love with my arrogant, annoying, sex god boss. Nope. No way.

Royally Fake Fiancé

The Duke of New Arcadia has an image problem only a fiancé can fix. And I'm the lucky lady he's chosen to play Cinderella.

Beauty & The Lumberjacks

After this logging season, I'm giving up sex. For...reasons.

Her Marine Daddy

My hot Marine hero wants me to call him daddy...

Her Dueling Daddies

Two daddies are better than one.

Innocence: dark mafia romance with Stasia Black

I'm the king of the criminal underworld. I always get what I want. And she is my obsession.

Beauty's Beast: a dark romance with Stasia Black

Years ago, Daphne's father stole from me. Now it's time for her to pay her family's debt...with her body.

ABOUT RENEE ROSE

USA TODAY BESTSELLING AUTHOR RENEE ROSE loves a dominant, dirty-talking alpha hero! She's sold over a million copies of steamy romance with varying levels of kink. Her books have been featured in USA Today's *Happily Ever After* and *Popsugar*. Named Eroticon USA's Next Top Erotic Author in 2013, she has also won *Spunky and Sassy's* Favorite Sci-Fi and Anthology author, *The Romance Reviews* Best Historical Romance, and *has* hit the *USA Today* list seven times with her Wolf Ranch series and various anthologies.

Please follow her on:
   Bookbub | Goodreads

Renee loves to connect with readers!
www.reneeroseromance.com
reneeroseauthor@gmail.com

ABOUT LEE SAVINO

Lee Savino is a USA today bestselling author, mom and chocoholic.

Warning: Do not read her Berserker series, or you will be addicted to the huge, dominant warriors who will stop at nothing to claim their mates.

I repeat: Do. Not. Read. The Berserker Saga. Particularly not the thrilling excerpt below.

Download a free book from www.leesavino.com (don't read that either. Too much hot, sexy lovin').

www.ingramcontent.com/pod-product-compliance
Lightning Source LLC
LaVergne TN
LVHW042202100225
803447LV00026B/222